# THE GENEALOGIST'S GUESTS

## Ann Simpson

Copyright © 2013 by Ann Simpson

All rights reserved. No part of this publication may be reproduced, distributed or transmitted in any form or by any means, including photocopying, recording, or other electronic or mechanical methods, without the prior written permission of the publisher, except in the case of brief quotations embodied in critical reviews and certain other noncommercial uses permitted by copyright law.

Publisher's Note: This is a work of fiction. Names, characters, places, and incidents are a product of the author's imagination. Locales and public names are sometimes used for atmospheric purposes. Any resemblance to actual people, living or dead, or to businesses, companies, events, institutions, or locales is completely coincidental.The Genealogist's Guests/ Ann Simpson. -- Createspace Edition

Our journey together is meant to be, for we are never separated by death.

# ONE

*Why didn't you turn the light on in there? You always set yourself up for the creeps.*

Elizabeth Ward did, and now she sat alone at her desk in her home office. Dark blonde hair lay on her shoulder. Her robe wrapped tight around her chilled body. The hairs on the back of her neck stood. She feels something lurking in the dark every night. She focused on her computer screen and saw something behind her in its reflection. She tightened her back muscles, squeezed her eyes shut, and whispered.

"Please go away."

She held her breath, opened her eyes and glanced back, and for a second she thought she saw something. Wood burned in the fireplace on the far side of the living room and cast shadows across the walls.

"Damn it Liz," she told herself. "Stop getting spooked."

She kept her grip on the familiar oval-shaped mouse and clicked on the database. She searched for the name Alexandra Hay. Her eyes were tired and watery, but there it was, a record of her great grandmother's arrival in America. A slight grin came over her face, then a frown when she saw her fifth generation grandmother had traveled alone.

The light from the only lamp in use flickered. She pointed the cursor to the, "favorite's star" on the screen, but the computer's hum went silent before she could left click. Before she could save the record the light flickered again, and shut off. The black screen reflected the fire behind her, and that of her own shadowed face.

"Fine, just fine." She sighed. "I'll find it later."

Liz stood and walked toward the fireplace, a second ago she thought something lurked in the living room. *Something lurked all right, your imagination,* she assured herself.

She poked the wood and poured herself a brandy. Looking around the space, she said, "I can't believe I've lived here alone for four years," and sighed. The only time she doesn't think about her isolation is when she's searching for ancestry records.

A tear trickled from the corner of her eye as she thought of her family she left in Virginia. Had they known what she did to her husband? *I doubt it*, she thought. But there was no going back to the stares and sneers of her past. She slumped on the sofa, rooted herself in the soft fabric, and cowered under her favorite throw. She listened to the creaking floors, and the rustle of papers from her home office. She dared not blink her eyes, not during the night.

Just before sunrise her eyes closed. Adjacent to the room, the home office door opened. The spirit of a woman wearing a white dress eased into the room and sat in the empty chair. Her eyes rested on Liz as she lay with her favorite throw draped across her body. Liz turned to her side and peeped at the empty chair. She blinked and took in a deep breath. *Go back to sleep, nothing is there.* She hummed, closed her eyes and allowed herself to drift back to sleep.

The spirit of Alexandra rose from the chair and hummed the same tune. Her ghostly orb hovered above the wood plank floor and moved delicate and slow across the fire lit room. She gazed back at Liz, and at the world of the living. Her visit made possible through Liz's hand-painted family tree, a portal to the afterlife. She entered the office where she reached her name on the family tree and disappeared.

Liz opened her eyes and lifted her head from the sofa. She spun around and glared at the empty chair.

"Goodness," she said. "Get a grip."

Through the curtains specks of dust floated about in the strands of light that reached across the living room leading to the office door. It was wide open. Liz dragged herself to her office and flipped the switch to the ceiling light. Nothing happened, no light, no computer.

She mumbled and opened the drapes. The sun peeked through and shined on the family tree. Liz swept her hair away from her eyes and smiled at her masterpiece. It took her months to hand paint each name and now it seemed her ancestors reached from their graves, through hundreds of branches to represent their place in time, their past lives.

"Excellent work Lizzie," she said.

An annoying screech startled her as she looked out the window. On the other side of the maple tree, across the long and narrow yard, tires rolled on wet pavement. Electricians jumped out of the truck and prepared to fix the broken link between their massive plant and Liz's house.

"It's time to get out of here," Liz said, and stomped toward the stairs. It was the third time in less than a month power had been lost in the house. Maybe they'll fix it right this time.

Outside, Randy Sullivan, a lifelong Rhode Islander peered at the property. Not a large man, but his piercing eyes intimidated most people. He stood behind the utility truck and waited for Liz to leave the house.

"Perfect," he said, as she finally drove away.

Randy loathed her living alone just as his mother did when she left him with his father. He was twelve when he found his mother and begged her to let him stay with her.

"No!" she had said to him. "Your father will come looking for you, go away!"

When he was old enough and strong enough, he escaped his father's beatings and many more rapes. The police looked for him unaware his mother lived close by and before they could arrest him he showed up at his mother's home. He watched her from the window with his father's blood on his hands, and his cold, empty eyes dead on her.

He climbed into the space as his mother watched television, and stood behind her as she laughed at the comedian. He grabbed her head and pressed the knife against her throat.

"You knew what he did to me, you bitch!"

Blood splattered through his fingers and across the television screen. He left her slouched body twitching as she bled out and never returned. He spent several years in a juvenile detention center for killing his parents. When he turned eighteen he was released, his record sealed.

Liz, he decided will be his next victim… of many. He had watched her for weeks after following her back from Norwich one Saturday. She was as she usually is, alone and vulnerable.

He sucked on his teeth and hollered to his coworker, "Danny, I'm going around back to check the lines."

"Watch for dogs," said Danny.

Randy glimpsed back and snickered at the way Danny struggled to get the toolbox open.

"That ought to keep him busy," he said.

He worked his way around the house peeking in each window until he reached the open back door.

"Ah, Ms. Ward, you're slipping," he said, and entered through the kitchen.

He crept past the refrigerator and noticed no sound came from it, and he knew there wouldn't be with the power out. But when he passed the clock and saw the second hand move, click, click, and saw the power cord detached from the wall. He said, "What the hell?"

He shook his head, his hands trembled, something told him to turn around and go back. He faced the office door and saw it move. It creaked and creaked until the walls vibrated. The door closed its gap, but stopped short of sealing its entry. Randy stood still, legs shaking. The stench of death filled the room. He finally turned to run like hell and as he did, the door swung wide open. He glanced back in enough time to see the door didn't recoil, as if something or someone held it against the wall. He wished his legs to move as he stood, staring.

The door slammed shut!

He sped out the back door and saw Danny by the utility truck. *Run, run*, he repeated in his mind until he finally found his voice, "Let's go!"

Danny had a big smile on his face as he watched Randy run toward him, he asked, "What's wrong? Did you find the dog?"

"You dumbass, get in the truck!" He rushed Danny and in one swoop shoved him in the truck and pushed him into the passenger seat. Randy looked back at the house, and saw nothing, but he told himself *go, go, go*, as he spun the wheels of the truck leaving the ladder behind splattered with mud.

Back in the house Alexandra's name faded next to her husbands on Liz's family tree. The whispers between the couple ensued.

*"Where were you Alexandra?"*
*"I chased an intruder away Dalton."*
*"Alexandra, where is Liz?"*
*"She's left the house."*
*"Go Alexandra, go with Liz. I'll watch the house,"* Dalton said.

The lights and refrigerator came on, the clock ticked, and the back door closed.

A few miles away Liz continued her drive until she reached the town of Norwich. She rolled her window down and took a deep breath. She passed the Wood River Cemetery and glanced back and read the name on the gravestone next to her ancestor. Church. She wondered if there were connections to the infamous Robert Church who was hung for conspiring with the enemy, and grinned, *Why not, after all, I am a descendent of someone who spied for the Confederates.* She asked herself what compelled a person to do such things, and then she burst out laughing.

"Shoot Lizzie what compelled you to leave Virginia?"

She thought back to her husband's crimes, his pedophile acts, her humiliation when it all came out as he lay on his deathbed. Her friends and some family members stared at her during the funeral. Their whispers quickly traveled around the room as the news spread. Her best friend's eyes were filled with accusation. Everyone scoffed as she edged toward the door of the funeral home. It hurts her to this day the way they all abandoned her after only a few days. She wiped the tear from her face and focused on her next turn onto Main Street.

The town of Norwich is never disappointing as it is rich with history. She parked in her usual spot and walked to the coffee shop. Along the way she bumped shoulders with a young lad and said, "Excuse me." He mumbled something and scurried on disappearing into the distance. She didn't see, that he disappeared and continued walking down the uneven pathway. The ghosts of many passed by, unnoticed, but they were there, sharing the walkways with the living.

# TWO

A breeze rushed past Liz as she crossed the threshold of the coffee shop. She stepped to the left side of the doorframe and squeezed through the small opening, a few steps before reaching the counter. She took a deep breath and relaxed, then glanced back at the door and watched as it slowly closed.

She turned and faced the counter and saw Louise wiping the coffee pot with a bleached rag.

"Good morning Liz. I have a fresh pot brewing." She tossed the rag in a bucket, then wiped her hands on her white apron trimmed in blue.

"I'll wait if you don't mind."

"It will be just a couple of minutes," Louise said, and reached for the bleached rag.

"No hurry," Liz said. Tickled.

She turned to the window and watched the town's people on the forefront of one hundred year old buildings. She wondered if Alexandra had come to Norwich from her Westerly, Rhode Island home and relished the idea that Alexandra would have seen then what she saw now before her. To her left a woman appeared to stroll the walkway. Her long green skirt with white polka dots brushed the sidewalk. Her overskirt swooped up on one side revealed an off white underskirt. Delicate hands extended out of cuffed fabric. Her face familiar.

*Alexandra?*

"Here's your coffee Liz."

Liz whipped her head around to see Louise's smile and watched her slide the paper cup across the counter, spilling the coffee. Louise grabbed the bleached rag from the bucket. Liz grinned and glanced back out the window. The woman in the long dress was gone.

"Thank you," Liz said. She rushed to the door, "See you next week Louise," she said and let the door close. She looked for the woman further down the sidewalk, but saw no sign of her.

She strolled around town and stopped in a few shops, humming that peculiar tune from the night before. She stepped out of the doorway of a thrift shop and there stood an old man leaning against the building. He nodded to her, a quaint hello of a nod. Liz smiled and went to walk away.

The man said, "Bells of Scotland."

Liz, stumped by the sudden remark said, "Excuse me."

"The song you're singing. It's called the Bells of Scotland."

"I didn't realize the tune had a name," she said.

"My grandmother used to sing it," he said. "She'd sit right over there." He pointed over to a set of steps. "I was a young boy, but I remember it all right."

Liz stared at the steps of the Town Hall, built in 1870.

"She wore her favorite green polka dot dress," the old man said.

Liz turned toward the man and said, "What did you say?" But he was gone. She stumbled back. *He didn't just say that.* She sprinted past Town Hall and found her car. *This is the crazy.* She unlocked the door and collapsed in the seat, swung her legs in and turned the ignition.

"I'm haunted."

"I can't believe I said that." She pressed her chest against the steering wheel trying to make sense of it all, she said, "Bells of Scotland." She threw the car in drive and sped out of the parking lot.

She reached her driveway and raced toward the house. "Good," she said after seeing the porch light. "The power's on." At the last second she pressed the brake and stopped a few inches from the back wall of the garage, swung the car door open and entered the

8

house through the kitchen. She stopped in the doorway, glanced over at the empty chair, and shifted her weight from one foot to the other and back, and darted toward the home office.

Through the computer screen, she saw her own shadowed reflection, she stepped back and found the lamp outside the office, "I won't make that mistake again," she said and pressed the switch. In the office she turned the lamp on and faced it toward her family tree, and stood there for a moment. *Bells of Scotland,* she thought as she scanned the names. Her ancestors came from England, Ireland and Prussia, and two from Scotland, Alexandra and her sister Sarah.

"I'm not crazy," she said. She spun around and plunged herself in front of the computer and pressed the power button. "Come on, load up," she said. "Coffee, I need coffee." She sprung up out of the chair and headed for the kitchen. The sun hadn't completely set and already exhaustion wore on her face.

Liz stumbled forward looking at the coffee pot and saw it brewed. She immediately looked over at the empty chair in the living room, threw her hands up in front of herself, and said, "Lizzie, you're losing it." She poured a cup of coffee and returned to her computer.

"An old folk song," she said, her voice low, "early 1800." She clicked on the next website and listened to a recording of the song.

She sighed and raised herself from the chair, cocked her head to the side, and stared at Alexandra's hand-painted name on the family tree. "This is crazy," she said. "I'm not haunted by Alexandra or any other ghost." She dragged her feet to the staircase, eyes tired. She paused and gazed around the room and at the window.

*It's still dark. Leave the lights on.* She told herself.

The ghost of Alexandra hovered above the wood plank floor at the base of the stairs Liz ascended. She scanned the room, *"I know you're here demon,"* she said. Her polka dot dress fluttered, her orb flashed, then stood solid, ready. Acutely aware of her purpose in the world of the living, to protect her great granddaughter.

\*\*\*

*Kill her.* The voices of many told Randy Sullivan. *She knows you killed them,* they said. He kneeled in the meadow and watched as Liz's bedroom light switched on, her silhouette moved across the room. *She's just like your mother.* The voice said.

"Leave me alone," Randy said, and stepped closer to the house. Dead grass crunched beneath his feet. He kept moving forward with one focused thought, dismember her.

\*\*\*

Upstairs Liz lay on her queen size bed with its foam mattress and oversized blue comforter. She stared at the window, a few more hours before daylight. She knew not to fall asleep before sunrise but a moment later her eyes fluttered back and forth under closed lids. Beads of sweat formed on her forehead. She tossed, side to side.

*"Wake up,"* the spirits said. *"He's coming."*

The blue comforter sunk to the floor, the top sheet floated above her momentarily before it whipped across the room. Ghostly hands pulled at her arms and legs. The face of an old woman appeared and hung above her, face to face. The old woman's eyes narrowed when she heard the dining room window raise downstairs, *"Wake up, girl!"*

Soon hundreds of spirits surrounded Liz, they cried, *"It's not safe, you must leave!"* Liz thrashed her arms, and pushed her attackers away. She gripped the fitted sheet and held tight.

*"Wake up! He'll be here soon,"* they said. Liz slept through their pleas, a nightmare she couldn't escape.

Downstairs, Alexandra watched as Randy Sullivan entered through the window. She hovered above him with closed fists. *"You will not harm my family,"* she said.

*"Is he a demon?"* the other spirits asked.

*"No,"* Alexandra said.

Randy kept moving, each step quiet as he climbed the stairs. He knew Liz's room was at the far end of the hall, facing the front lawn.

*"Leave."* Alexandra said. She whispered close to his ear.

Randy missed a step and fell forward, his palms on the stair, head facing down. He closed his eyes.

"Shut up," he said.

He squeezed his eyes shut, lowered his head and reached for the next stair. Alexandra pressed down on him as he continued his low crawl toward the top of the stairs. Five maybe six rapid voices at times screaming inside his head, *kill her!*

When he reached the top step the voices stopped. He got to his feet. His eyes squinted. The quiet hall offered one light that peeked from under Liz's bedroom door. He stood, leery. Where did the voices go? He took one step and the floor creaked. He looked down toward his feet, closed his eyes and took a deep breath. He opened his eyes.

*"Leave!"*

The floor shook.

"A woman," Randy said.

He scowled, moved forward and pushed Liz's bedroom door open. The stench of death rushed toward his face and he saw Liz levitating three feet above the bed. A fierce white cloud twirled and circled around her.

"Run!"

The voice was his own. He stumbled back, turned around and saw a woman suspended above the floor. He darted across the space to the top stair. Alexandra moved fast and was right behind him. He gasped at her distorted face and stepped back off the edge of the first stair and tumbled. His arms flailed back, his palm hit the fourth stair down, and the weight of his body shattered his limb. On the final stair he heard a snap in his neck. Fluid gurgled in his throat. He saw his right foot and knee facing down on the last three stairs, the rest of his body faced up.

*Move.*

A mixture of saliva and blood spewed out of his mouth, again he looked at his legs.

*Move.*

The eerie sound of his inner voice was useless. He gazed at the woman hovering above him until his listless stare went blank.

***

Liz woke up with her lower half body hanging off the foot of the bed. She looked around and saw she was alone.

"A dream Lizzie, just a dream."

She remembered enough about the dream to know someone tried to take her away, but she fought.

She giggled, "I must have been fighting hard to end up down here," she said. Her heart beat fast and faster as she looked over at her bedroom door and saw it closed.

"Oh no!"

She scrambled to the phone and dialed 911.

"Please help me," she said. "Someone is in my house!"

"Ma'am stay on the phone, we'll send an officer."

"Please hurry."

She stared at the door handle. *Please don't turn.*

Downstairs in the office the tree shined bright at first, then dimmed as each of Liz's ancestors made their way back through the branches, the portal back to their graves. Alexandra stood at the office window until the headlights from the police cruiser appeared at the end of the long dark driveway. By the time the police entered through the back door, she too joined her clan. The tree shimmered and then went dark as everyone again was at rest.

Liz stayed at the foot of the bed, and breathed into her blue comforter, staring at the door handle. The phone was at her ear.

The emergency operator said, "Ma'am the cruiser's in the driveway. Are you still in the bedroom?"

Liz stood keeping her eye on the door handle. She took a couple of steps toward the door. She took a deep breath and swung the door open, and braced herself for impact, then saw the way was clear.

"Go!" she said, and then darted toward the stairs.

She passed the door of another bedroom on her left.

*Don't look Lizzie.*

She tilted her head toward the right and reached for the handrail, and gripped it tight. She got her first look down the stairs. Randy's body lay at the bottom, eyes wide open and blank. Her upper body jerked, her legs locked. Lights flashed across the room and came to a stop on the dead man. Liz whimpered.

"Police, Ma'am."

"Is he dead?" she said still holding the rail tight, only now with two hands. The officer shined the light on her face. She squinted her eyes and tried to focus on the officer's face. Relieved, she couldn't see the dead man.

"Is he dead?"

"Wait right there, ma'am," the officer said.

She leaned her body against the staircase and looked away.

"Are you sure he's dead?"

The officer reached the top of the stairs, he said, "Can you tell me what happened here?"

"I don't know. I woke up half way off my bed." She stuttered, "I had a bad dream."

Liz looked into the young officer's eyes, and saw the same expression as her friends and family in Virginia, when they thought she knew about her husband's pedophilia. Her thoughts were rapid. She glanced down the stairs, dead eyes stared back at her, and she could swear those eyes knew she killed her husband.

Another officer topped the stairs and whispered to the first officer. Liz looked around for an exit and quickly realized the only way out was down the stairs, down past the dead man whose accusing eyes were fixed on her. Sweat beaded across her forehead.

*They're going to arrest me.*

The officers stopped talking; both turned and looked at Liz.

"It's not confirmed yet, ma'am. But we think its Randy Sullivan. A couple of investigators were over at the community mental health center just this morning inquiring information on him."

Liz kept blinking her eyes, trying to gather her thoughts.

"But why is he here?" she said.

Another man reached the top of the stairs. He was dressed in a suit with a tie; he introduced himself and offered a handshake. Liz reached for his hand, a detective; she heard that part but missed his name.

"We're not sure ma'am. But the other victims lived alone too. Maybe that's why he chose you," the detective said.

Liz ignored the dead man's stare and focused on the detective. "Other victims?" she said.

"Yes, ma'am, we think he's responsible for several homicides in the area."

Lights flashed through the curtains downstairs, reporters swarmed the front lawn. Liz silently prayed the dead man would stop staring.

# THREE

It's been weeks since Liz encountered strange happenings around the house. The media stopped harassing her about the dead body found in her home. She remained there most days lost in research connecting each piece of evidence she found to her online tree. A New England cold snap was all it took to avoid the town. She decided to wait for a thaw before attempting to walk around Norwich. She had piles of wood delivered for the fireplace. She closed off all doors to rooms she intended to vacate during the winter months. Her thermostat was set at sixty-eight, chilly by her standards, but she kept a fire going and had her sleeping quarters next to it.

Liz sighed, as she stood looking out at the white landscape. It was beautiful, how the snow glistened in the sunlight. Two feet of it had fallen on top a foot that already lay on the ground, unable to melt due to extreme temperatures. She slid her snow boots on and targeted her mailbox. She trudged through the weight of the snow keeping her eye open for footprints or any other signs of an intruder. A routine she developed after her encounter with a serial killer. She reached her mailbox and banged the top with her fist to loosen the ice.

"Well, now Lizzie, don't go breaking your hand," she said as she rubbed the pain away.

She pulled the oval shaped flap. Her hand slipped and gashed the side. Her blood dripped on the sparkling snow. She walked away to trudge her way back to the house, and then it happened. She heard the crack of ice and the squeak of the hinges. The wind rushed into the mailbox and sent her mail flying across the landscape. Liz shook her head slow and stepped back. She watched a single envelope float in the air and land at her feet. Looking down, she saw her blood dripping beside the envelope, and then the name of the sender. She snatched the envelope up and headed for the house, a trail of blood followed.

She shielded her face from the blistering snow as she approached the house and stopped in her tracks when she saw the front door was open. Her heart pounded in her chest, she thought the wind must have blown the door open. She had no choice but to get her bleeding under control. She dashed into the house and made her way back to the kitchen sink.

"Liz, see what you've done," she said as water cascaded over her hand.

She held the dish towel over the wound until the bleeding stopped and went upstairs for bandages leaving the letter behind on top the kitchen counter.

The family tree lit up as the apparitions made their way to the kitchen. Chats of company arriving in the spring began with enthusiasm. Upstairs Liz wrapped her hand with gauze. In the winter months, it would take emergency personnel an hour to get to her. Aggravated with herself, she walked to the staircase. She heard something and stopped at the top of the stairs, and listened.

*Whispers.* She thought. *Someone is down there.*

In the kitchen, excitement over visitors grew among the spirits, but when Liz reached the bottom of the stairs, the room went dead silent. She didn't remember adding wood, but there it was, a fire kindled to perfection. She walked into the kitchen where her blood remained in the sink, the letter next to it.

"Don't let this be bad news," she said.

Before she broke the seal, she read it again, the senders name and address, Abigail Cook, Alexandria, Virginia.

She used her elbow to hold the letter in place on the counter as she ripped the glue apart and pulled the letter out of the envelope. Two pictures fell to the floor. Liz sighed and unfolded the letter.

She heard a whisper behind her and turned to see who it was, and when no one was there, she said, "Stop it Lizzie."

She read the first sentence of the letter.

"We're coming to visit!"

Tears formed as she continued to read, "They'll be here in the spring," she said aloud.

She half expected a response as she cried over the news. She retrieved the photos from the floor and in them a beautiful baby girl. They named her Clara after Liz's great grandmother. She read further and they'll bring her new great niece along with them. She hasn't seen her family in nearly four years, four years of being isolated, for the most part in her small home office with not the memories of her living relatives but visions of her ancestors. Strange, if not eerie visions she'd love to forget.

Liz laid the letter and pictures on the counter and gawked at the blood, her blood. She had an awful thought about dying alone if something should happen to her.

"Goodness Liz, stop it already," she said. "No use getting all emotional. Its company, that's all."

She steadied her breathing as she wiped the blood up until all was clean, and then she wailed, loud, right there on the kitchen floor until she heard music. Liz grabbed a dish towel and held it to her sobbing face as she stepped toward the office. Just as she got to the doorway, the music stopped. Her computer was on the web page she had found with the *Bells of Scotland*.

She sighed and said, "You left the computer on again Lizzie." Then wiped her face and said, "Time to prepare for visitors."

Making her way upstairs humming as she topped the stairs, she saw sunlight. The doors to the bedrooms, all four were open. She stood in the hall and looked into each room. No one slept in the rooms in four years. A good washing was in order, she thought, and so she took all the bedspreads downstairs and placed them next to the washer. She would shop for essentials when the weather cleared, and have the interior painted.

In the home office, the ghost of Alexandra said, *"Remember Dalton, remember when Sarah came to visit?"* Her name on the tree flickered as Dalton spoke from his place on the tree next to her.

*"Dear you worry too much."*

*"No Dalton, remember she brought that stranger with her."* Like a lighting bolt Alexandra's painted name lit up fast and fierce. *"He was a killer!"*

*"That was a long time ago,"* Dalton said. His painted name lets out a soft sparkle. *"One's upset, isn't one? Let's concentrate on the gathering, shall we,"* he said.

Just then Liz walked into the room, she heard people talking again.

"I'm not crazy," she said.

Yet, she talked to no one. She had heard it before, the whispers around the house, but each time she dismissed it, now she felt someone next to her lurking in the empty space, her knees weakened, she took a deep breath, she thought, *perhaps waiting for the perfect moment to attack.*

"Darn it Liz, don't get yourself all worked up over nothing," she scolded. The likelihood of a ghost being in the house was impossible, she told herself that, and as she focused her energy on planning for her guest, it dawned on her. Randy Sullivan died in her house.

"Oh come on Liz," she said. "There's no way Randy, the ghost is here!" She decided being alone was getting to her, and the idea of company, real guest from Virginia played with her mind.

She walked over to the lamp by the office door and turned it on, and stumbled back toward the kitchen. At the bottom of the staircase, a dark misty cloud hovered over the wood floor. Liz gawked at the sight and kept stepping back. She could not take her eyes off what appeared to be a man in her living room. She stepped to the right thinking she could get out the door and to her car. The stench gagged her. The figure shifted to its left. Then the lights went out, but Liz could still see it looking right at her. He moved again headed straight for her. A low, menacing snarl accompanied him. He's coming after me, she thought. She let out a cry and moved around the kitchen counter. She had to get out fast. Sweat beaded at the top of her forehead and dripped down the side of her pale face.

She gasped for air and kneeled as he lunged forward. She leaned back on the counter and screamed. Something moved near the office door. Liz held her hand to her chest tight. A large transparent cloud swished from the office and surrounded her would be attacker. She ran through the back door to the neighbor's house, two miles away. Her bloodline remained, each apparition attacking the evil intruder until it was gone.

*"Dalton,"* Alexandra whispered to her husband.
*"Yes, Alexandra."*
*"He'll come back."*

# FOUR

Liz kneeled humming away as she watered the soil under her blue violets and other flowers in her garden.

"Good morning Liz," George Southworth said, appearing behind her.

"Good morning George."

"Liz, Margaret and I would like you," he stuttered, "to come for supper later. Say around seven."

George and Margaret had been there for Liz when she had her episode, as they called it, during the winter months. Margaret has since sent George over to Liz's property every other day to check on her. Liz looked up at him as he towered six feet, and three inches, "I'd love to come for supper George. What can I bring?"

"Funny you… should ask Liz," George had a sly grin as he helped Liz to her feet. "You've been doing some baking. I can smell… it over at my place." He smiled and raised his brows.

Liz laughed and said, "George, I'll bring an Apple Pie, how's that sound?"

"I can pick you up if you like."

"Oh, that's quite all right." She smiled. "I'll be there at seven."

Liz was thankful for her new friendship with her neighbors, without them, she would not have survived that cold winter day when she fled her home. George found her lying down by the roadside in the snow about a quarter mile from his place. It took Liz two weeks to go back home after the incident. By then the snow had melted and Liz was able to drive her car. She felt comfort knowing she could drive away at the first sign of trouble. She eased up on her ancestry research blaming the entire incident on extreme hours of computer use and secretly blaming it on loneliness. She dared not tell anyone about her visions for fear they would think she was crazy.

George climbed back into his white Ford pickup truck. He looked back at Liz as he rolled along the driveway and faced forward, and got a glimpse of a man in the tree line. He slammed on his brakes, causing the gravel to stir. Liz stood by her flowerbed watching the peculiar way he moved around in his seat. That's when George saw Liz watching him through his rearview mirror. He threw the truck in gear and got on out of there. Liz searched the tree line and saw nothing, except it was a beautiful scene. In fact, her land looked as if someone had manicured it to a perfect setting.

"How splendid," she said. "My guest will approve," talking in grandeur style.

George wasted no time getting home to Margaret and when he charged through the door screaming, "It's just what… you said Margaret! She has some spirits over there. Saw it with my own eyes!" Margaret was not surprised.

"Calm down George," Margaret said. "We'll help Liz. Now tell me what you saw."

Known throughout New England as the one who talks to spirits, Margaret's well versed on the afterlife.

"There was a spirit standing on her property. He…disappeared, right before my eyes."

"He's not a threat." Margaret looked motherly with graying hair and a round jolly face.

"Margaret, how… do you know?"

"He's watching Liz."

"What shall we do Margaret?"

"I think it's time to tell Liz about me over supper tonight." She said with a joyous tone. She always sounds joyful, even when she plans to hold a séance. Margaret grabbed a bag of potatoes, and began pealing, once done, she snapped green beans, and fried pork chops, by that time the table was set when Liz walked in and laid her fresh baked apple pie beside the mashed potatoes.

"Wow, this is a surprise. Everything looks so sophisticated, is this your best China?"

"It was my mothers, and yes, Liz it is my best."

"It's beautiful Margaret," she said sincerely. "So what's the occasion?"

"Well, Liz since you asked. We invited another guest. A man named William Church. He's a long time friend of Georges, widowed a couple years back."

Liz tried to hide her excitement, but the smile on her face gave it away. She asked, "Has his family been in Rhode Island a while?"

"Why, yes the Churches have been here for many generations. Why do you ask?" Margaret's head tilted as she stared with an inquisitive expression on her face.

A knock on the door interrupted their chat. Liz's arms swung upward. They looked at each other and sighed as George said, "Bill, what... the hell took you so long? Come this way I'd... like you to meet Liz our neighbor from across the way."

Liz looked over at William Church. *He is gorgeous*, she thought, and then realized her mouth was wide open. He was maybe mid fifties, her age, and he stood a good six feet with broad shoulders and black hair with just a touch of gray. He stared at her during the entire greet. Liz brushed her hair away from her face. Margaret, of course, noticed and directed everyone to the table. George seemed more nervous than usual; knowing what Margaret was up to made him nervous.

He said, "Liz has... been next door for about four years now Bill."

"Yes, yes," Bill said, "I know, she came up from Virginia in the spring. I was happy to see someone move into the old house."

Liz had a perplexed look on her face, she asked, "You're familiar with the house?"

"Yes, I am," Bill spoke with authority. "My family built it in nineteen hundred after a fire destroyed their old place over in Westerly."

Liz shifted in her seat. She lives in Bill's family home and she may have some ancestral ties with him, if she's correct about his family being buried in the cemetery with her ancestors.

She snapped out of her own thoughts and finally asked, "You mean the house was yours?"

Margaret already felt the ties between the two. She also felt a presence. George passed the pork chops followed by mashed potatoes and dinner rolls, appearing busy to his guest. He glanced over at Margaret, who nodded her head letting him know there was a presence.

"You know Bill," Liz couldn't resist. She said, "I moved here to research my family history and up in Wood River Cemetery, where many of my ancestors are laid to rest, I saw the Church family. Any chance they're related to you?"

Bill leaned back in his chair. His grin was as handsome a grin Liz had ever seen. She hoped she wasn't blushing, but by the look on Margaret's face, she knew it was obvious. Liz suspected a match making in the works and she felt her face blush more with the thought.

"Liz, I didn't know you were searching your family history here," Margaret said. George smiled at Margaret. She knew darn well what happened over at Liz's place.

"To answer your question Liz," Bill interrupted. "Yes, that is my family."

Margaret saw an orb behind Liz. Its colors were dark and Margaret could sense its turmoil. She couldn't quite figure out who it was, just yet, but it seemed disturbed.

"We may be connected Bill," Liz blushed at her choice of words. "I mean, I think we may have ancestral ties." Bill's grin excited Liz and he could tell too, and saw no reason to stop putting on the charm.

"I heard some tell of a Church marrying into the Ward family," he said. "A male named Winston Church. Yes, he married a young lady named Mary Ward."

Liz leaned forward and with a serious look on her face, she said, "Yes, that was in the early eighteen hundreds, wasn't it?"

"Well, now you do know your family tree. Perhaps Margaret here can help us with this puzzle."

Liz looked at Margaret, not wanting to take her eyes off this delicious man, but she was curious enough to ask, "Margaret, you do ancestry research?"

George cleared his throat as Margaret scooped up a fork full of potatoes. As she laid the fork back on her plate she said, "Not exactly Liz."

"What do you mean?" Liz asked.

George interrupted this time. He said, "Liz, Margaret is… a medium."

"Medium" she shook her head, "I'm sorry, please explain." Liz's attention was on Margaret now.

Margaret's round face with her rosy cheeks, and delayed response spiked Liz's curiosity.

Bill said, "Margaret's."

Liz raised her hand, "Shush," she whispered and waited to hear it from Margaret.

Bill tickled at Liz finally busted out with, "Margaret can talk to the dead." He sat back amused at the expression on Liz's face.

"It's true," he said. "In fact, if I know Margaret well enough, we have a spirit with us right now." His voice was calm and direct as he nodded to Margaret.

"Now Bill," Margaret said. "You're going to scare her."

"Perhaps it's time for… some of that good smelling pie you made Liz," George said. He always did get anxious at times like this.

"It's ok. I'm not afraid." Liz said. Then she asked a peculiar question, "Margaret you know, don't you?"

Margaret watched the orb flash back and forth as if it were going crazy. Liz, Bill, and George couldn't see it, but Margaret couldn't take her eyes off it. Liz saw her looking over her own head and she turned to see for herself. Bill leaned back in his chair. He saw this many times before, but his attention wasn't on Margaret's odd behavior, it was with Liz. He was slowly or perhaps quickly, hell he didn't know which was accurate, but he felt infatuated with Liz. She seemed in good health, self-composed, and authentic, a good old gal.

Margaret announced, "Incoming!"

About that time, the orb passed by Liz's head and struck Margaret knocking her out of her chair. Liz jumped up and made her way around the table.

She said, "Oh dear, are you all right!"

George went for the candles, a chore he was accustomed to, and the moment he lit the candles the lights went out.

Bill let out a laugh and said, "Pie by candle light sounds great!"

Margaret got herself back into the chair and said, "That one there was a pistol."

"Are you all right, dear?" George's hands shook as he reached for Margaret's arm. His face was red as he clung to her.

"I'm alright," said Margaret.

Liz saw the affection between them, a reminder of her own loneliness, but it was beautiful the way the two cared for each other. She glanced over at Bill and since he had been staring at her all evening she wasn't surprised to see him looking at her.

"Bill," Liz said. She looked back at Margaret, and back at Bill again. "You've seen this before." She looked back at Margaret, "Margaret, you're a medium? I mean you talk to spirits. You know there are spirits in my house, don't you?"

Margaret sliced the pie as she spoke, "About a month after you moved in Liz, I could feel something going on, I wasn't sure at first. When George found you down by the road I was sure."

"What made you sure?" Bill questioned, always the curious one.

Margaret looked at Liz. "When you stayed here with us, they were here too."

Liz sat back in the chair. She looked over at Bill. His eyes fixed on her.

He took a bite of pie and said, "Good pie," with a grin on his face.

George smirked.

Liz looked at Margaret, she said, "There are spirits in my home and they followed me here?"

"Yes, Liz they weren't any harm." She said blissfully. "I felt they were watching over you, perhaps protecting you. But…"

"But — what?"

"There's an evil presence Liz."

"You mean the one here now?"

Margaret's rosy cheeks deepened. She said in her motherly tone, "No, that one's following Bill."

Bill choked on his pie and then cleared his throat. George laughed.

"Liz we'll have a séance over at your place," Margaret announced.

George stopped laughing.

"These ghosts, I don't know who they are, or why?" Liz said. "I mean strange things happened but it's not like a ghost has walked up and said something like 'Hi, how you doing?'"

"Perhaps you weren't ready," Margaret said as she cleared the table. "Perhaps they are compelled to show themselves somehow. There is a doorway, an opening between our world and theirs. The doorway or portal linked to you is how they come; fear, sadness, danger, or pain awakens them. Or," Margaret paused.

"Or, what?" Liz asked, enthralled with Margaret's knowledge.

Margaret leaned back contemplating, she half spoke to Liz but more so to herself, "Maybe an old piece of furniture or memorabilia, something that reaches back in time."

Liz leaned back in her chair collecting her thoughts. The thought of going home to a house full of ghosts made her palms sweat.

She said, "Margaret, mind if I stay here tonight?"

"You're welcome to stay anytime Liz."

Bill took a swig of tea and clanked the glass down on the table, "Now that that's taken care of, Margaret, please tell me about this orb following me."

# FIVE

Liz had the table ready for the séance by the time Margaret and George arrived.

"Bill should be here any minute," she said.

She grabbed some candles and placed them near the table. George stood back out of the way with a wide grin on his face. He's seen many people prepare for séances' only to find out later that chaos is inevitable. The three stood around the table waiting for Bill. Liz used her apron to dry her sweaty palms and then threw it on the counter. She took a deep breath and as she exhaled, she heard someone moan.

"What was that?" Liz said.

Her face whitened. George looked pale and blue. Margaret had a concerned expression as they each took a step toward the staircase. Every time the wind blew, or the house creaked, or the nothing in between their fear intensified.

"What the hell are you doing?" Bill said, standing behind them.

Margaret sighed.

George snapped, "Bill, don't you sneak... up on us like that!"

"Easy George," Bill said. "I didn't intend to scare you. What were you doing? You were acting like you saw a ghost."

"There was a strange... sound. It came from upstairs," George said.

Bill laughed and said, "Perhaps the wind. It is breezy out there. Feels like a storm approaching." He sat a bottle of wine on the counter.

"Planning on a party Bill?" Liz asked, her tone sarcastic. The color returned to her face, her arms folded across her chest.

Bill grabbed both her shoulders.

"Yes."

His smile drove Liz crazy with desire.

"Liz now don't you worry. I've seen Margaret handle troublesome spirits. We'll be all right."

Bill gave her one last squeeze and let go.

Margaret listened but she wasn't sure this time. The spirit that haunted Liz clearly wanted to harm her. His presence prickled the hairs on her arms and neck.

"Liz perhaps we should wait before we hold a séance. I think I'd like some time to further investigate." Margaret spoke with a seriousness that even George hadn't seen in a while.

"Margaret, please. I have my family coming soon and I'd like this problem resolved before they arrive. I fear something awful will happen. Please Margaret."

The four stood around the table. George didn't feel good about this one. Bill stared at Liz. He couldn't help himself, with each part of her lips he yearned to touch her. He thought about her since their last encounter at George's place, her strong confidence, her good ole ways, as he sees it she's an exciting woman. He felt sexually alive, literally bulging with desire.

A loud bang startled the four, something rustled across the floor upstairs.

Margaret looked up at the ceiling and asked, "Where did that come from?"

Liz said, "Upstairs somewhere."

"Is that what you heard?" Bill asked.

George stepped toward the staircase, and felt cold air. He darted his eyes and balled his fists. Something evil hovered and growled.

"George," Margaret whispered. She heard it too and more, she noticed a stench. The odor grew stronger with each passing second and caused Liz to gag. She covered her nose and mouth. The foul smelling apparition appeared before them. Upstairs something dragged across the floor. They all heard it, but said nothing. It wasn't furniture or any other hard surfaced item. It could be a mattress from one of the beds, but that idea eliminated when they heard a woman's cry.

The ghost of Randy laid his evil eyes on Liz.

"You leave her alone! Leave this house!" Margaret said.

Behind them, in the home office, the branches of the family tree swayed. The ancestors remained trapped on the other side, the portal closed. They watched the scene unfold from the afterlife. Their cries were unheard by Liz and the others.

*"Dalton."*

*"Yes, Alexandra."*

The sound of Alexandra's cries awakened all the others. *"It's happening again,"* she whimpered. *"Dalton, he took my son."* Alexandra's pain, a pain only a mother could feel nearly crippled her in 1885 when a stranger took her only son at age seven.

*"Come now, dear, Dalton Jr. is here with us now."* Dalton had spent a lifetime soothing his wife, and in death, his loyalty remained.

*"Dalton, he's after Liz now,"* she whispered.

Wood River Cemetery, some three miles west of the house was quiet, one would say a deafening quiet. Many of Liz's ancestors lay to rest on the grounds dating back to the seventeen hundreds. A bloodline of strength and love, a family united, even in death. The storm approached. Thunder shook the grounds. A wave of angry souls stirred as the family attempted to reach Liz from their graves.

The staircase shook behind the evil entity. The apparition moved closer to Liz. Her hand painted tree lit up like lightening in the other room. Each ancestor's cries grew louder behind Liz's masterpiece. Liz reached for George. The ghost's eyes narrowed. Thunder clapped sending a vibration strong enough to shake tables. A vase fell to the floor and crashed into several pieces. Liz did not take her eyes off the evil ghost now inches from her face.

Margaret yelled, "Leave her alone!"

The spirit lifted her from the floor and flung her across the room. She landed by the fireplace.

"Margaret!" said George.

He ran to her side, leaving Liz and Bill by the stairs. Bill reached from behind Liz and held her shoulders. Randy's evil soul turned to Bill. It twirled around him, forcing him to move away from Liz, and stopped when Bill was up against the wall some four feet away. Liz stood there watching Bill's face twist, he moaned pitifully.

Liz said, "Please, leave him alone!"

Randy's wicked apparition turned its attention to Liz.

"Please leave." Her words inaudible to everyone except the evil before her.

The thing moved closer to her.

"No, no, no!"

She thought of her family tree and all the people she'd join in death and the living she'd leave. Randy's spirit struck her and backed away. He prepared to strike again, and thrashed forward.

Liz screamed, "Alexandra!"

Alexandra's spirit burst through the branch at a speed only the dead could accomplish. Her ghostly figure raised above the floor. Her long white dress trailed behind her. Her eerie screech startled Liz. Loyalty ran in her blood and it belonged to her husband and their family. The way he stood by her as she mourned the death of their son. The love they shared. Her strength supported by the backing of her family, a gift passed through a bloodline. All her being, surged toward Randy.

The grounds of Wood River Cemetery opened, releasing generations of anxious spirits from their graves. At the front of the house an apparition on a horse appeared wearing a Union Soldiers' uniform. He came with weapons ready to fight for his descendants. Behind him in the tree line Benjamin Ward, the farmer, and Mary Jordan Ward, his parents appeared, he with a hoe in hand and she with the backing of her bloodline, her parents and their parents. One by one, they all came screeching from their graves heading toward Liz and her call for help. However, none were as fast as Alexandra, the fiery spirit of Scotland.

Randy held Bill to the wall, and Bill felt helpless as he watched Liz plead. George held Margaret tight and tried to hide her face from the terror. Nonetheless, Margaret saw as she peered over George's shoulder. Alexandra moved in fast, and was a blur until she stopped in front of Randy. Margaret felt her anger, love, and deadly intentions. Liz saw the second ghost and screamed louder. She didn't know her call brought the raged female to her, and to Randy. Alexandra's screams intensified as the seconds on the clock next to Liz ticked. Liz watched the two ghost's face off, the noise harrowing, she couldn't move.

The evil spirit let Bill go when the second ghost appeared. As the two ghosts hovered a couple of feet above the floor, he crawled underneath trying his best to get to Liz, who sat against the opposite wall, her face frozen in terror. The clock next to her continued to tick the seconds away and the sound of each passing tick grew loud and louder until the walls shook. As the seconds continued, the two ghosts Liz watched went silent, each facing the other. Liz held her palms over her ears and saw Bill crawling toward her and then looked back at the female ghosts. The deadly expression Alexandra had when faced off with Randy gave way to an adoring expression when she looked at Liz.

Across the room, Margaret saw the connection between Liz and the female ghost. She felt Randy's malicious spirit; in fact, through his eyes, she saw Liz and the female apparition. It occurred to Margaret the female is Alexandra. Margaret closed her eyes and allowed herself inside Randy's thoughts. He was morbid. His anger directed at Alexandra. The last tick of the clock, during the dead silence, Margaret knew he intended to attack.

She yelled, "Alexandra!"

Alexandra's spirit shot up high toward the ceiling, but the vengeance was hers as she came back down and sped around Randy faster and faster. The attack was violent and more ghosts appeared from the family tree, each attacking Randy. A man on a horse appeared dressed in a soldier's uniform. Liz recognized him right away, or at least he looked like the man from the corner store in Norwich. The Civil War Veteran paused for a moment, smiled at her and disappeared into the brutal cyclone with the others.

# SIX

Liz got to her feet and steadied herself against the wall. Her dark blonde hair mangled, clothes twisted. Bill, Margaret and George looked about the same, like they went through a twister.

"I can't believe this," Liz said as she looked around the room. A second before a fierce fight between the serial killer and her ancestor abruptly ended, both apparitions disappeared, to where she had no idea.

George helped Margaret get to her feet, she more anxious than he to get to Liz. She dashed across the room excited she said, "Liz, are you all right?" She and Liz both looked around at what they expected to be a mess. Everything in the room, a war zone seconds before, was intact. "We don't need a séance now." Margaret said with a wide grin.

"The clock, Margaret, did you hear the clock?" Liz asked.

"Hear it! My ears will ring for weeks!"

"Hey, everything… looks normal," George said, scratching his head.

Bill laughed and said, "Everything except you three."

Liz asked Margaret, "Is it over?"

"For now, I think."

Bill was the first to hear the music coming from Liz's office. He took a couple of steps closer to Liz. He opened his mouth to say something.

Liz whispered, "Bells of Scotland."

Bill whispered, "What?"

"It's coming… from your office Liz," George announced.

"I know it always comes from there."

Margaret's jolly grin returned, "You've heard it before Liz?"

The four inched their way toward the office, huddled together. Margaret led the way. They stopped short of entering the office and all four leaned forward, peeking into the space. The means from which the music played wasn't identified at first, but as it faded, everyone turned their heads facing the family tree.

"A masterpiece," Bill whispered.

Liz whispered a thank you as they all stood before the tree reading the hand painted names. Continuing with the whispers Liz reached her hand and pointed to Alexandra's name.

"It was her," she said. "She's my fifth generation grandmother, Alexandra Hay from Scotland."

"Liz, in all my years, all the times I used my psychic abilities to contact the dead, I've never seen anything like this." Margaret spoke like a mother consoling her children. She said, "Your tree Liz, it enables your kin to come from the other side."

Liz went to speak, but gasped instead. All four quietly pondered with amazement the idea of Liz's ancestors coming through her artwork.

A popping sound behind them startled each one, but none turned to see what caused the sound. Instead, they each turned their heads and looked at each other. Another pop followed by a series of bubbly sounds.

Liz said, "It's coffee."

Bill asked, "Coffee?"

"Yes,"

With narrowed eyes Bill said, "Who exactly made coffee Liz?"

"I think there's a short in the electrical wiring. It starts brewing on its own." Liz whispered the answer as the four walked into the large living area and faced the kitchen.

George said, "Margaret and I have… an electrical short like that too. It's called a timer Liz."

"My coffee maker doesn't have a timer George."

"Oh," said George. "Maybe it's a short in your… wiring."

Margaret said, "Maybe it's your ancestors Liz."

"My dead kin come from their graves to brew my coffee?"

Bill interrupted, "Why not we just saw them attack an intruder."

"Oh, this is too much!" Liz said. "I have family arriving the day after tomorrow."

"I have a feeling they won't scare your family away Liz. They're protecting you. I don't believe they'll appear unless there's a need to protect you from harm." Margaret rubbed her hands together. "You must tell me about your ancestors."

Liz stared down at the floor and ran her hand through her hair. She had no choice; she had to stay in the house. She looked up at her guests and grinned, "Coffee, anyone?"

"Yes, I'll have coffee," said Margaret.

Bill and George glanced at each other. "I think… I'll have some of that wine Bill," George isn't a drinker, but the past hour left him thirsty for more than coffee. Bill was happy to accommodate and join him. They came together in the large living room and sat facing the fireplace.

"There's a… chill don't you think," said George. A spark in the fireplace produced a single flame. George said, "No way." More flames burst. George's hand shook as he poured another glass of wine for himself and Bill.

"Margaret, I didn't know too much about my ancestors, who they were or even their names until I researched them. I now have a tree nearly three thousand strong."

Margaret isn't interested in how Liz got into genealogy. She wants to hear about her ancestors themselves, but she patiently waited for Liz to tell her story. She nodded her head.

"I came here to research them. I love the area and since building my family tree was my hobby, I decided on Rhode Island and Connecticut, because my ancestors are from here. I searched for a home to purchase." Liz looked over into Bill's eyes, "I fell in love with this house." Liz felt her cheeks blush.

"Liz, tell me about your research. What did you find out about your ancestors?" Margaret was eager to learn more. George grabbed the wine bottle.

"Well, there's a lot to tell if you're interested."

"I am," said Margaret.

"George, Bill, how about something stronger? In fact, why don't we all have something with more kick?" Margaret grabbed the bourbon and ice.

What an evening it was, after a few drinks, everyone felt relaxed, the fire warmed the living room and all was tranquil. George tried to forget about the ghosts, it's what he wanted to do, but unlike his normal inability to connect with the dead, being the goofy sidekick to Margaret during previous séances, he now felt their presence.

"So Liz," Margaret said. "Tell me about your ancestors? Tell me about this Alexandra." George poured himself and Bill another drink. Bill leaned back onto the sofa and stared at Liz. He wanted to hear about her findings as much as Margaret did, but more so he wanted to hear her voice. The alcohol he consumed gave him courage, though Bill didn't lack courage while sober, he felt more daring after a few drinks and he certainly wasn't hiding his affection for Liz.

"She arrived as a young girl, I found, just sixteen." Liz said as she settled onto the sofa next to Bill.

"The one record I have," Liz eager to tell her story, cleared her throat, she said, "shows she came without family or at least anyone with her surname, Hay. She came from Scotland, her homeland before she boarded the ship California bound for the US in 1875. She married Dalton Luther Ward two years later. He was from Rhode Island. The Ward family had already been in the New England area since the 1600's. He and Alexandra had a son they named Dalton A. Born in Connecticut. He died in Rhode Island, a month before his eighth birthday."

Fighting tears Liz said, "I can't imagine the pain Alexandra suffered."

"Liz your ancestors, Alexandra and the rest appear through your tree. It is mysterious but not unheard of; there have been other cases where deceased family members are sighted. However, yours protect you from harm. I have no doubt they were involved with the serial killer's death when he broke into your house that night." Margaret said, "I cannot sense their presence at the moment."

George sat in the chair, staring behind Margaret. His eyes were teary. The ghost is barely visible. He saw how beautiful the spirit had once been and as Margaret talked about not feeling the presence of ghosts there's one staring at him.

Margaret said, "I'm sure they are here and I suspect my dear husband can see them."

The comment took George by surprise. He cleared his throat and reached for his drink on the coffee table. He said, "It's... unsettling dear, but it's not evil. I feel sorrow."

"How many George," asked Margaret?

"Only one," said George. "The same one Liz... calls Alexandra I think."

Bill looked over at George, "George," he said, "You can see them?"

"You... sound surprised Bill."

"Yes, I am surprised. You never told me you could see them."

"I couldn't until... recently. Margaret dear, what does this mean?"

"I'm not sure George, but I think she knows you aren't any harm to Liz. When Liz screamed for her earlier, she flew through that office door squealing like a banshee, like something evil. She's powerful. She's watching over Liz, protecting her from harm."

"Excuse me," Bill spoke up, "Why does Liz need protection?"

"Good question Bill. There's trouble ahead, I think."

"What do you mean there's trouble ahead, Margaret, I can't do this now," Liz's hand shook as she sat her glass on the tabletop. "I have family arriving. I haven't seen them in four years."

Bill gave Liz a strange look, he asked, "Margaret tells you," his voice dropped deep, "You have ghosts in your house and you're worried about your family coming to town?"

"I see your point Bill but I've lived here for four years and up until that serial killer I haven't had any problems."

Bill let out a hardy laugh, "Your coffee brews on its own, we've sat here for what two, three hours and the fire we never kindled to begin with hasn't dwindled, your great grandmother who died in

1917 stands behind Margaret, and not one of us has had the nerve to get up and use the facilities."

Bill leaned his back against the sofa. His grin drove Liz crazy. She didn't know what to say and for a moment she just stared at Bill's face. Margaret cleared her throat and jolted Liz back to this world.

"Bill," Liz said with a grin of her own, "Would you be so kind as to escort me to the bathroom?"

Bill smirked, "I would my dear, but I'd have to stand outside the bathroom door alone."

George was half-drunk. When the laughter burst out he sprayed a mouthful of bourbon across the room. Margaret laughed too and covered her mouth but the drink escaped and spilled into her palms. Bill felt it coming on and he tried to hold it in but let out a snort followed by an uncontrollable laugh. The bourbon went down the wrong pipe causing him to choke.

"Bill, are you all right?" Liz reached over and beat Bill on his back. He kept on laughing as he tried to clear his throat. Liz laughed too but tried not to because she could barely hold her bladder.

"George, old fellow tell me something," Bill nodded his head to where the presence was last seen, he said, "The guard?"

George looked across the room, he said, "Hey, where'd she go?"

The four sat silent and searched for the ghost of Alexandra. It's soft sounding, the flip of the light switch. They heard it and each turned around and saw the bathroom light illuminated across the hall floor.

# SEVEN

Liz stood in the doorway, "They're about to pull into the driveway any moment Bill. Did you check on the pie? Did you turn the lamp on by the office?"

Bill walked up behind Liz and put his arms around her, with his calm voice, he said, "Everything is perfect Liz." The scent of Liz's flowers breezed by with the wind.

"I haven't decided," Bill said.

"Decided what?" Liz turned to face Bill. They looked into each other's eyes, and moved closer.

Bill pulled away and said, "Which smells better, your flowers or that sweet smelling apple pie." Liz laughed, and Bill nodded his head toward the driveway. When Liz turned to see she saw the dark maroon minivan with her family inside, each stretching their necks to get a look at her.

"Bill," Liz's voice quivered.

"Yes."

"Bill how do I look, I forgot to check myself."

"You have flour on your chin and you forgot to take off your apron."

Liz raised her hand to wipe her face, but Bill intercepted.

"You're most beautiful as you are right now. I'll load the suitcases in after the introductions and then I'll be on my way home. I'll see you in a couple of weeks after your company...."

"Oh no you won't, you stay right here with me!"

Bill laughed, he said, "As you say ma'am, where am I to sleep?" His grin thrilling.

"You and I will sleep on the living room floor and watch the office and hope the ancestors stay rested beyond the tree."

"You mean stay dead don't you?" Bill smirked.

"Liz!" Abigail yelled from the van.

The family piled onto the lawn, each getting their hugs from Liz. Bill stood back out of the way. After a while he felt left out if not uncomfortable until he looked down and saw a beautiful little girl with curly light brown hair and gorgeous brown eyes. "Hello," he said.

"Hi, my name is Elizabeth, Mary Elizabeth, what's your name?" Her voice squeaked.

"Well now Mary Elizabeth, my name is Bill."

In her cute little girl's voice she said, "Please to meet you Mr. Bill."

"Elizabeth is wise beyond her three years." A stunning female with the same features as Liz, dressed in low-rise jeans, spaghetti string top, and a bright yellow jacket extended her hand to Bill.

"Hello, I'm Abigail, Liz's niece."

"Hello Abigail," Bill extended his hand to her.

Out on the lawn standing alone is a man they call Stan. He lurked in the background. Bill continued his greets and offered to bring luggage in as Liz showed everyone around the house. The stranger never approached Bill, never offered his hand.

The home office door remained closed. Inside the ghosts of Alexandra and Dalton stood at the window facing out, their spirits cautious and discreet.

*"Dalton, he's not one of us."* Alexandra warned.

*"Who are you speaking of Alexandra?"*

*"That one, the one they call Stan."*

*"Why Alexandra, why is he not one of us?"*

*"Dalton, remember when we let the stranger in our home. Remember Dalton, what he did to our son?"*

*"Our son is with us now Alexandra."*

*"We'll watch the stranger. You go now, go enjoy the family,"* he said.

The office door opened and Alexandra left leaving Dalton behind with the others. Their whispers started before he returned to his name on the hand painted tree.

*"Alexandra is right, Dalton. There's trouble ahead,"* they said.

Dalton remembered back in 1885. Winter neared, the air brisk. He and Alexandra were busy preparing for company. Little Ed, seven years old, ran about on the front lawn when his Aunt Sarah Hay arrived with her new friend, Wilbur Savage. Sarah was Alexandra's younger sister and she was smitten with Wilbur. She didn't know that Wilbur's family feared him; she didn't know he preyed on little kids, and that he killed as many as four in a few years.

Dalton remembered all right, the horror of finding his son, dead down by the river. The search team of about thirty, Alexandra and Sarah included, and Wilbur, he was there too. They scoured the area for hours. It was Dalton, who found young Eddie. At first, his cries were silent, looking down at his only son, his only child, bloodied about the face. He searched Eddie's body from head to groin and it was there he saw the pool of blood expelled from his naked lower half and that was when he realized his son had been viciously raped. That was when his cries were no longer silent.

He remembered as if it was yesterday seeing Alexandra, run at a speed he thought impossible, and when she reached him and their dead son. He remembered the horror on her face, her trembling hands as she reached for her son. She picked up the necklace her sister, Sarah, made for Wilbur Savage.

Dalton remembered the moment two sisters separated for life when his Alexandra wailed to Sarah, *"You brought that stranger to my home!"* Sarah changed forever; she never married, never again left her home. He remembered his own savage revenge on Wilbur, when he sliced him with the blade repeatedly until Alexandra stopped him.

On the other side of the painted tree in the afterlife Sarah Hay said to Dalton, *"I am here for you, brother in-law."*

Dalton remembered how he took her food every week, how he cared for her and his wife until his death.

Behind the painted tree he said, *"There's trouble ahead. Call the family."*

*"We're here Dalton,"* they whispered, hundreds of them from as far back as the late sixteen hundreds, his grandparents Dalton and Mary Phillips, and Joseph Ward, the one they called the most gentle man there ever was and his wife Abigail Havens. Liz's niece named after her. She's the one who said it first, *"We feel it to Dalton."* The news spread fast in the afterlife as Alexandra watched her descendants join upstairs.

Bill piled luggage onto the entryway floor. He walked toward a chatty conversation he heard near the staircase. He peeked around the corner and there stood young Mary Elizabeth looking up at Stan.

She said, "But I'm going to sleep with Great Aunt Liz."

Stan towered over her. His lean stature, domineering and threatening, his voice demanding he said, "You will sleep where I tell you. You understand."

Mary Elizabeth hung her head, her hands dropped to her side. Bill was careful not to let Stan know he was there. He didn't know how Stan fit into the family, but guessed he's Abigail's boyfriend by the way he talked to Mary Elizabeth.

In her weakest voice Mary Elizabeth said, "I understand."

Stan left her standing there alone, and took two stairs at a time to reach the top. He never looked back. Bill saw Mary Elizabeth cry and then watched her as she kneeled down and ran her petite fingers through a small puddle of her own tears on the wood plank floor. When she stood up Bill hurried into Liz's office and hid from her as she walked by the door. He noticed her slumped shoulders and the way she nearly dragged her doll. Minutes before she had hugged the doll close to her heart, but as she passed by the office door it seemed to burden her, as if the weight was too much to carry. Bill watched her until she disappeared through the kitchen and out the garage door. As he stood in the doorway of the office, a ghostly figure stood behind him. Bill felt odd and turned to see the room empty and just then Liz and her family descended the staircase.

Abigail let out a squeal after slipping at the bottom.

"There's water on the floor," Abigail said.

Bill's eyes followed the cascade of people up to the second landing and saw Stan behind everyone else. His brow wrinkled as he grabbed some paper towel and handed it to Abigail, and watched as she unknowingly wiped her daughter's tears from the floor. He sat the roll of paper towel back onto the counter and saw out the window Mary Elizabeth twirling around out on the lawn. She stopped dancing for a moment and then shook her head yes, then sat in the meadow. He shifted his eyes back to Stan and stepped to the side to get a better look, his gaze probing.

"I have an idea," Bill announced. "How about the kids sleep down here, camp style. Liz and I will be down here anyway. I have sleeping bags over at my place. We can roast marshmallows and tell ghost stories

Liz said, "Maybe we won't tell any ghost stories!"

"Ok, no ghost stories," Bill laughed at Liz and then adored the way she stood there holding four months old Clara.

Abigail added, "Ok, but Clara will sleep with me and Stan."

"Oh Abigail you've traveled far, let her sleep down here, you and Stan can get a good night's rest." Liz said.

Stan looked furious, but Bill didn't care. Liz caught Bill's sly grin and wondered what he was up too.

"Where's Elizabeth?" Abigail had just realized she wasn't there.

Bill said, "I saw her outside a couple of minutes ago." Mary Elizabeth hopped across the grass and hugged her doll tight. Bill looked across the room and saw Stan in the living room window staring out at her. Beside Bill was Sarah; her apparition hadn't left his side.

She whispered to the others, *"The one they call Stan, he's evil."*

*"Where's my Alexandra?"* Dalton asked.

*"She's there, out in the meadow with the children. She's happy Dalton,"* Sarah sighed.

*"There's trouble ahead,"* they all whispered amongst each other.

Alexandra watched the children playing about on the lawn. She watched Stan too, as he looked out the window. She knew the ugly truth about his intentions, to harm little Mary Elizabeth. She and the other spirits waited for trouble to begin. All dead eyes were on Stan.

"How would you like to give me a hand with the sleeping bags?" Bill asked Stan.

Stan dropped his shoulders and rolled his eyes.

"Sure."

"Good then we'll leave in a moment," Bill said, and then walked away and left through the garage. He pulled the phone out of his pocket and fumbled with it before he reached Margaret. "Margaret ole gal, I think we have some trouble over here at Liz's place."

"I know Bill, there's darkness all around Liz's property. Bill there's something else."

"What is it?"

"It's George. He's not feeling well. He's been in some kind of trance. I believe it has something to do with Liz's troubles."

"It's the one they call Stan, Margaret. I think he's after young Mary Elizabeth, I just feel he's going to harm her."

"Bill, Liz's ancestors won't let that happen. Besides, I feel Alexandra's power from here. I can't read what she's planning, but…"

"But what, Margaret?"

"Bill there's something more going on over there, something dark and sinister."

"Margaret old gal, get George out of that trance and come on over. I'm taking Stan to my place to pick up some sleeping bags. I need you two to watch over Liz while I'm out."

Liz saw Bill from the window talking on the phone. She saw when Stan joined him out in the driveway. She watched as they both left in the car. She heard the laughter of children playing over in the field, *there should only be Mary Elizabeth*. She gazed out the window again.

"Impossible," she said aloud. A young transparent boy was over in the tall grass. A ghost, and as Liz realized who the boy was, she had to catch her breath. She whispered, "Young Eddie Ward, Alexandra's son."

# EIGHT

Liz slept in front of the fireplace to keep the children away from the flames during the night. Bill lay closer to the bathroom next to the stairs so that if Mary Elizabeth woke and went into the bathroom, he would know, and more important, he wanted to protect her from Stan. He didn't tell Liz about his suspicions of Stan, thinking she'd be better off not knowing, unless it became necessary.

Bill dozed off until he heard a sound upstairs. He opened his eyes and stared at the ceiling, waiting to hear movement. After a while the noise stopped and he dozed off again.

In the corner of the room, quiet and mysterious, Alexandra's spirit hovered. She watched the children sleep. Her posture rigid, her orb jerked back and forth. Her intuition told her Stan did not belong in the family. She stood guard until the morning hour, protecting her bloodline. She watched Mary Elizabeth climb out of her sleeping bag. She tugged at Bill's blanket to wake him.

"Hi," said Mary Elizabeth.

Alexandra was looking at Bill at first, until she realized Mary Elizabeth was talking to her. She flew back to the corner. Mary Elizabeth jumped up and down.

Bill threw his sleeping bag to the side. "What is it Mary Elizabeth?" he asked.

"Who is that?" Mary Elizabeth asked, and pointed to the corner. Bill didn't see anything but he knew, or suspected it was a ghost. He hoped a friendly one.

"I don't see anyone sweetheart."

Mary Elizabeth smiled at the woman ghost she saw lingering in the corner. Bill watched her carefully and though he couldn't see what she saw he felt as though the ghost meant no harm.

"Good Morning."

Bill jumped a foot off the floor. Mary Elizabeth giggled at him. Margaret stood at the bottom of the staircase laughing.

She asked, "Seeing ghosts?"

Bill came back with, "No, no ghosts here." He looked at Mary Elizabeth and said, "Let's start breakfast shall we." He picked her up and headed for the kitchen. Margaret followed. As they walked away Mary Elizabeth waved her small hand goodbye to the ghost she saw in the corner.

"She can see them," Bill said.

"Yes it appears she can," said Margaret.

He sat Mary Elizabeth at the kitchen counter and whispered to Margaret, "I don't know how long I can keep this from Liz."

"Keep what from me?" Bill turned to see Liz standing right behind him. He fumbled his words as he tried to come up with something to say.

"Liz," Margaret interrupted. "It's about Mary Elizabeth."

"What about her."

"She can see the spirits."

"The spirits, I thought they were gone."

Margaret moved closer to Liz, "It's not a problem Liz. Children are more open to the other side than adults."

Liz said, "Yesterday I thought I saw a young boy playing with her. I didn't say anything. I don't know why. I feel like I'm losing it. Like I don't know what is real anymore." Liz looked around for Mary Elizabeth.

"Where is she?" Liz searched for her. She found her standing in the corner of the living room looking up into open space. George came running down the stairs and halted at the bottom and stared at the same corner.

"Mary… Elizabeth, come over here," he said.

"What is it George," Margaret asked.

"It's... Alexandra."

Daylight peeked through the windows and shined on Mary Elizabeth's small frame as Alexandra's bright orb hovered above her in the dark corner. She reached her petite hands toward the woman ghost she saw before her. Liz and Bill only saw Mary Elizabeth reaching high toward the corner of the room, but George could see both child and the spirit of her seventh great grandmother. He remained quiet and watched as Alexandra's ghost leaned toward Mary Elizabeth allowing her tiny fingers to touch her face.

Margaret stood in the kitchen watching the event when suddenly her eyes rolled back into her head and her hands extended straight out in front of her round body. She stood trapped in a trance and as she channeled its energy, she felt its cold flesh, smelled its putrid odor. It traveled through her body, hissed like a snake. Its tongue slithered in and out of its mouth.

"Liz," Bill said and then pointed to Margaret.

"Oh my, Margaret," Liz said, clutching to Bill. "What's happening?"

Mary Elizabeth reached for Alexandra's face. All of a sudden the orb started pacing back and forth, shifting from one corner to the other. Mary Elizabeth took a couple of steps back. The ghost of Alexandra thrashed against the walls, unable to escape. Inside the home office on the other side of the family tree Alexandra's husband, Dalton, and her sister Sarah heard her cries.

*"What is wrong with my sister?"* Sarah said to Dalton.

*"She's afraid,"* said Dalton.

*"Of what?"* Sarah said.

The evil spirit cocked his head to the side and saw Dalton coming. It looked back at Alexandra and snarled. Then rushed back through Margaret, back to the underworld.

Alexandra's pace slowed as her husband and sister joined her in the corner.

*"What has scared my sister brother in law?"* Sarah asked.

*"A mean spirited Boggart, Sarah,"* Dalton said.

*"But Dalton... who?"*

George grabbed Mary Elizabeth and watched the three orbs fade away.

"Bye," Mary Elizabeth waved her hand as George held her in his arms. George saw his wife rising from the floor. He sat Mary Elizabeth down. Liz helped Margaret up and joined Bill and George in the kitchen.

Margaret said, "He came without warning. He's evil, more evil than Randy." She spoke with a low voice so that Mary Elizabeth couldn't hear her.

"Do you know who he was?" Liz said.

"No Liz, I don't. I didn't feel him coming either."

George moved closer to the conversation, he said, "Alexandra's ghost bounced off the walls when it came. I think… she was afraid."

"Any sign of Randy?" Bill asked.

"No sign of him," Margaret said. She hadn't felt him around the house.

"This new one," she said and then paused.

"What is it Margaret?" Liz asked.

"Liz he's more evil than Randy, and more powerful. I could smell him and feel his snake like tongue in my own mouth as he passed through me."

"What do they want," Liz said.

She held the kitchen counter tight. When she spoke, she had to catch her breath. She could not wrap her thoughts around anyone, alive or dead, wanting to bring harm to her family.

"Liz something about the new spirit scared Alexandra. There must be a history there, possibly something tragic." Margaret said as she grabbed a glass of water.

"All right," Bill spoke with a sense of urgency. "We are all on ghost watch." He reached for the eggs in the refrigerator. Liz grabbed a pan. Margaret and George pitched in as well. Together they prepared breakfast as Mary Elizabeth played on the living room floor. She didn't give Alexandra's ghost another thought.

At the top of the stairs, Stan was crouched behind the banister. His sights were on Mary Elizabeth. He had watched her from her bedside many a night, waiting for the right time to touch her. His patience wore thin. He had to have her, control her. She resisted his every attempt to gain her trust. He'd snap at her when she pulled away from him. Yet he kept trying, and as he strove to make Mary Elizabeth his, he had to pretend to want Abigail. He loathed

Abigail's every touch, couldn't stand to sleep in the same bed with her, and could barely wait to see her face when he and Mary Elizabeth announce their commitment to each other.

Mary Elizabeth didn't notice Stan kneeled at the top of the stairs at first, as she played on the floor. Bill watched her from the kitchen. He saw when she looked up the stairs, when her angel face frowned. Bill took a couple of steps to his right and peered up the stairs confirming his suspicions.

"Ok everyone, come into the kitchen for breakfast," Bill announced. Mary Elizabeth was the first to jump up and run toward him. He thought it was sad, how Mary Elizabeth grabbed happiness, every little bit, she could in between the fearful moments when Stan was near. No child, he thought, should be in such a situation.

Bill captivated Liz. She could not take her eyes off him. She watched him as he interacted with the children. He was kind and funny, patient and watchful.

*Watchful,* she thought.

He watched the children like a guard. She was just about to let her curiosity go, thinking, of course, he protected the children; they had ghosts popping up everywhere, for goodness sakes. Then Stan entered the room and she saw the look on Bill's face and the way he moved closer to Mary Elizabeth. Everyone exchanged good mornings, everyone except Bill.

George said, "I'd like to take the children to my farm, they can pet the animals and I can do my chores."

"That's a wonderful idea George," said Liz.

Overwhelmed by the last few nights she welcomed the idea of the children having fun.

\*\*\*

In the home office, the family tree was quiet, at least on this side of the tree.

Deep into the ghostly afterlife turmoil spread fast. Darkness had fallen upon Alexandra, her moans reached decades of ancestors disturbed by her cries.

*"Why do you cry my dear,"* Dalton said, looking down upon her.

Alexandra's hair was out of its neat bun, her eyes sunken, as she lay on a bed of blue violets unresponsive.

*"Brother in law, tell me please, what is wrong with my sister?"* Sarah said.

*"I know not what bothers my wife Sarah."*

Wilbur Savage's plan worked. He lured Alexandra's soul into his personal death den, his realm in the underground. Hundreds of dead tree branches covered her face and body. His drool was thick and black. It poured out of his mouth and dropped just beneath his chin and then twirled and spun upward back into his mouth where his snake like tongue slithered out.

*"Tell me Alexandra, where is your son."* he said.

Alexandra shrieked. Her eyes remained closed, trapped under Wilbur's curse.

Dalton stood over his wife in his realm; her spirit disappeared and quickly returned.

*"Go sister in law."* He said. *"Go see what ails my wife. She may disappear for good."*

The ghost of Sarah faded into the background until it was gone.

# NINE

Margaret sat in front of Liz's painted tree studying the names. She had been quiet since the foul demon used her to go after Alexandra. She examined each male name hoping to find who the unexpected visitor was and why he went after Alexandra. It was hard to find evil in the tree. Liz had created it with love; her passion imprinted each branch of the afterlife. The names sparkled as she searched for a sign, for anything that would help her understand. She examined each name all the way to the top of the tree and then followed them back down to the base and was stunned at what she saw. Alexandra's name, it looked old and dead among the live and vibrant names that surrounded it.

"Oh my Alexandra," Margaret said. "You are in trouble."

"Who is Alexandra?"

Margaret's hands flew up in the air and the stool she sat on tilted. She grabbed the floor lamp beside her. She landed on the floor with the lamp rested on top of her. Abigail rushed in, "I'm so sorry. I didn't mean to scare you."

"That's quite all right, dear." Margaret said, looking up at Abigail, "Would you lend me a hand?"

Abigail helped her up and they stood in front of the tree.

Abigail said, "Oh, I see, you were looking at the names. It's beautiful isn't it."

"Yes, yes it is quite beautiful. Alexandra is here." Margaret pointed to what appeared to her as a dead tree branch. She watched Abigail's face to see if she had the gift but Abigail didn't seem to notice the difference between the branches, she didn't see Alexandra's dilapidated name.

"Let's see now," she said. "Alexandra would be your sixth great grandmother. Liz tells me she was from Scotland."

Abigail smiled and said, "Interesting." She looked at Margaret never losing her smile, she said, "Let's join the others shall we."

As they walked out of the office, Margaret looked back at the tree of names. She saw Alexandra's name, a dead limb with no connecting family names, except one, the one called Sarah.

"We saw all the animals!" Mary Elizabeth rushed into the main room screaming.

George followed with a huge grin on his face. Bill gave him a pat on the back, "Huge success I gather," he said.

"It was hard pulling... her away from the farm," George said, with a goofy smile on his face. He walked over to Margaret and put his arms around her shoulders. She stared off into space. He expected her to smile at his fun loving disposition, but she seemed preoccupied. "Are you all right... dear?"

Margaret didn't respond. Instead, she watched Liz's interaction with her nieces. George looked over at Liz and then at Bill, who watched Liz as well. Looking back at Liz, George saw how caring she was, a true gem. On the other side of the room, he saw a female ghost, that of Sarah. He clasped his hands together as he stared into her ghostly eyes. He tried to look away.

Margaret nudged George, "What is it, dear?"

"Another... female, she's here."

"I believe her name is Sarah," Margaret said.

"What does... she want?"

"I'm not sure, but it has to do with Alexandra, her sister."

"Margaret she looks... worried, like she's trying to tell me something."

"I believe Alexandra's in trouble, but she's blocked me so I can't see what it is."

"Can't see what?" Bill said.

Margaret and George both jumped.

"Look old… fellow, no more sneaking up behind people!" George's strong whisper made Bill smile.

"It… isn't funny," George snapped.

Bill laughed and gazed across the room. He saw Stan holding Mary Elizabeth's hand walking out of the main room. Everyone else was piled in the middle of the living room floor laughing and having a good time.

He yelled at Stan. "You leave her alone!" Pain shot through his stiff neck, he had enough of Stan.

Liz saw it, the look on Stan's face, the guilt. Margaret saw something more, Stan's dominance over Mary Elizabeth.

Stan stood in defiance. Mary Elizabeth was his and he did not intend to allow Bill or anyone else take that from him.

"What the hell is going on?" Abigail said as she moved toward Mary Elizabeth.

George saw the ghosts, many of them scattered around the room. "Oh… dear," he said.

"Mary Elizabeth, go to your mother," Bill said. The ghost of Sarah suspended in the air behind him.

Stan's growl was deep and eerie, he said, "How dare you interfere with us."

Abigail moved fast. She grabbed her daughter and held her close. "What have you done?"

"You!" Stan sneered at Abigail. "You pathetic bitch!"

Bill grabbed Stan by the lapels, "Mister, you have crossed the line!"

Stan threw a few punches to Bill's face. The impact didn't faze Bill. He raised Stan up off his feet and threw him to the floor.

The spunky apparition, the Union soldier stood close by throwing shadow punches. Stan struggled to get up and made it half way before Bill planted a solid punch to the side of his head. He fell back to the floor, but then rose to his feet, prepared to fight.

"Get out of my house!" Liz said.

George stood in the background looking at the spirits gathered around Bill and Stan. Chaos gripped them as well. The ghost of Sarah was close to Stan, and when he lunged at Bill, she raised both her hands and pushed him back. Her power threw Stan several feet backwards. Bill looked back at Liz making eye contact and both knew what had just happened. Liz grinned. She thought, *that's my ancestors.*

Stan scrambled to the front door. He gazed around, but his eyes looked distant.

"Get out of this house!" Bill said.

Liz stood behind him surrounded by her family, the living and the dead. Stan opened the door and walked away without saying a word.

Abigail held Mary Elizabeth close. "I feel like such a fool," she said. "Aunt Liz, we have no where to go now. The house in Virginia is Stan's."

"You always have a home, dear. You and the children will stay here for as long as you need or want. I would love to have you here." Liz said.

"Aunt Liz. Really?" she asked.

"Oh dear child," Liz said. Before she could say more, Abigail jumped in her arms. Bill was all smiles as he watched them cry together and then laugh.

Bill placed his arms around Liz's shoulders, always the skeptic, he said, "So, when you are going to tell her about them?" He nodded his head toward Mary Elizabeth, who stood facing the corner of the room smiling at what appeared to most as nothing but empty space. Liz gave him a sharp strike to his side with her elbow.

"In time," she said. She walked into the office and stared at her family tree. Alexandra's name appeared limp and much like death.

"It's been like that for some time now Liz." Margaret said. "She's in some type of trouble, Liz."

"But who," Liz's voice cracked. "Who pushed Stan?"

"I suspect that was Sarah, Alexandra's sister. She's come to warn us I think."

"Warn us, about what?"

"See Liz, that's what I don't know."

They stood there before the tree wondering what trouble lay ahead. The sound was as familiar as an alarm clock's buzz. Margaret and Liz stepped out of the office and saw everyone gathered around the television.

The weatherman announced the threat of bad weather. A monster storm ahead, he said as the red warning scrolled across the screen. High winds, rain, floods likely, and widespread power outages. The words he spoke were not nearly as threatening as his tone. He rushed his speech as if the report would end at any moment. The screen switched over to the radar. Indeed, a monster storm headed straight for them.

"It looks like we'll be bunkered down here for a while." Bill's sly grin was back.

Liz smiled and said, "I have a cellar. If we need to we will go there."

"We have a few hours to get everything ready," Margaret said.

"I have… to go tend to my animals," George said as he ran out the door. George enjoyed the simple life as much as he could after his retirement from law enforcement. He spent his days tending to his small farm and a much smaller garden. With the threat of bad weather, he knew well he would have to get all the animals inside the barn. He turned the engine of his pickup and drove until he reached the end of the driveway. Across the way in the maroon minivan, Stan sat watching George.

"I'll bet you're going to tie them animals up." He started the van's motor and followed George. The wind had picked up a few notches. Dark clouds diminished the daylight; rain had just begun to fall. The porch light at George's place barely helped light the area but Stan could see George as he walked toward the barn. George swung the barn doors wide open and entered the large space. He finished the chores and jumped back into the pickup to head back to Liz's when he saw the minivan. He looked inside the van creeping around like a burglar the entire time. It was empty and he didn't see Stan anywhere, but when he looked back at his place, there in the kitchen he saw a light. He could hardly believe it; it had to be Stan in his refrigerator.

"You… little scoundrel," George said as he made his way to the front door. Now George was a good man, never caused anyone trouble. His good police sense told him not to enter without his sidearm. He recalled the last time he saw his sidearm at the station the day he retired.

"I won't need this anymore," he told the captain.

He crossed the threshold and entered his house. He heard a shuffle like a drag of someone's foot and then he heard Stan's breath. Stan jabbed the cold steel into his side and twisted the blade.

"I won't allow you to interfere." Stan said.

George fell to the floor never seeing his attacker. He lay there bleeding. His last words, "Margaret, I love you."

# TEN

They huddled together by the fire satisfied they would weather the storm. Abigail kept Mary Elizabeth close as they talked about the old days of when Liz still lived in Virginia. Coffee started brewing on its own and caused a stir, but Liz announced she had a short in the electrical wiring. Bill giggled at that one. Everyone was there except for George. Over in the corner where Alexandra was last seen stood Sarah, though no one could see her, she still had that worried look in her ghostly eyes.

Margaret burst out with tears. Her fists balled and arms stretched.

"What's wrong Margaret?" Abigail said.

Mary Elizabeth ran to Abigail and stared back at Margaret. Liz and Bill rushed to Margaret's side. A loud crack of thunder followed by power disruption left the living room lit only by the fire. The office door slammed wide open. Abigail and Mary Elizabeth screamed.

"It's just the wind," Bill said. He kneeled beside Margaret and grabbed her leg.

"Margaret old gal, what's wrong?"

Margaret stared at the corner of the room where Sarah was. A light appeared in the window and made its way into the living room. Sarah levitated high in the corner: her stare haunting.

Abigail winced at the look on Margaret's face, she said, "Someone please help her."

Margaret's tears flooded her face and soaked her clothing beneath her chin.

"Margaret please let me know what I can do." Liz said.

Abigail noticed Margaret's unrelenting stare at the empty corner in the room. "What the hell is this?" she said.

"We don't know Abigail." Liz snapped.

Margaret said, "G... George," her voice a cry of agony.

Bill looked at the corner and saw nothing but when he looked over at Liz and saw her expression, it hit him, hard.

"No, no, no!" His friend, his lifelong friend, it can't be.

"Oh dear God, Margaret," Liz held her close. They stared at the corner, crying and hugging each other.

Abigail stood up and walked near the corner of the room. She looked at the empty space and then back at Margaret. "Wait a minute," she said. "You see ghosts?"

"That's why he could see them, that's why, that's why...." Margaret chanted.

"Them?" Abigail said, "Ghosts?"

Abigail stomped across the floor. "Is this house haunted?"

"Abigail! Not now!" Liz said.

Abigail through her arms up, "Aunt Liz I want to know is what hell is going on around here!"

"It's George, Mommy." Mary Elizabeth pointed to the corner. "Hi George," Mary Elizabeth said as she waved.

George's spirit hovered above Mary Elizabeth. He looked adoringly at his wife as she repeated, "George, George."

Margaret continued to mumble words as she rocked back and forth. Bill listened to her and when she said Stan killed George, he shook his head, "No," he said. He knew it had to happen over at Margaret's place. He stood, his chest rising and falling with each breath.

"Bill?" Liz said.

Before he walked away, before he charged out the door, he said to Abigail, "You take care of everyone! I'm going for Stan!" Abigail threw her hands up in the air and then slapped them on her thighs.

"Oh! That's all right Bill I can take care of it," she said. She stood there for a moment thinking it was crazy, Bill, going after Stan on his own.

"Aunt Liz," she said. She looked at Margaret and then over to the corner of the room where Margaret had not stopped staring.

"Ok," she said, "I have to go help Bill." She looked at Liz, "Whatever this is," she said as she pointed to the corner and ran out the door.

George's truck was near the house and beside his truck was the maroon van.

"You son of a bitch, you're still here," Bill said.

He parked away from the house and walked toward the only light he saw coming from the kitchen. He saw Stan through the window. The way he helped himself to Margaret and George's food, the way he propped his feet up on the table took Bill by surprise. He watched Stan carry a conversation with a doll that sat across the table from him.

"You sick bastard." Bill said. The storm brought with it a lot of wind. He walked around the front of the dwelling, rain beating his face.

"Bill."

Bill froze and waited.

"Bill," Abigail said. "Bill, what are you doing," she whispered.

"Look here young gal, you get back home," Bill said.

"Bill, this is crazy. Let's call the police."

Bill put his hands on the side of the house and hung his head. He knew Abigail was right. It was crazy.

He said, "You're right." He nodded his head, "Let's get out of here. We can call the police once we are down the road a ways."

He threw his arm around her. When they turned to walk away the impact of Stan's fist blinded Bill. Abigail caught him as he fell back against her. She helped him back to his feet and there in the heaviest downpour yet she saw Stan standing with his legs wide apart, his left hand down by his side, and his right holding a shotgun. He looked half-crazed.

Abigail said, "Come on Bill, let's go!"

Stan raised the gun and pointed it straight at them. "Get inside now!"

Stan walked them through the front door. Bill choked up when he saw George's body lying in the front hall. Abigail held Bill close, she said, "I'm sorry Bill."

"It's not your fault Abigail."

Stan shoved them toward the kitchen.

"Shut up! Both of you!"

They entered the kitchen and there Bill and Abigail saw the table set for two and a doll at one end.

Stan said, "Mary Elizabeth we have company, Bill and your pathetic mother."

He grabbed Abigail by her arm and forced her to sit at the table. "We have something to tell you… bitch."

He shoved Bill to the floor. Bill's head hit the cabinet and left him with a small gash on his forehead. He stayed on the floor; afraid Stan would hurt Abigail if he tried to do anything. "You have been one annoying bitch," Stan said to Abigail.

"Stan you need help," she said.

"Shut up!"

Abigail held her head down and faced away from Stan. Bill saw how afraid Abigail was and said, "It's all right Abigail."

Stan rushed at him and kicked him to his side. Bill fell over in a fetal position as Stan stomped him to his body and head.

"Stop!" Abigail said. "Leave him alone!"

Stan paused and took a couple of steps back. In between breaths, he let out a scream. His face was red and his neck veins bulged as he held his head high and then he slammed his fist on the table.

Looking at Abigail he said, "None of this would have happened if it weren't for you! You had to come here. You had to see your poor lonely Aunt Liz!" He laughed and said, "Turns out she wasn't lonely at all! Isn't that right Bill. You've been screwing that old bitch all along! I don't know how you do it; touch her. I can barely stomach touching Abigail."

He faced Abigail, "You're old and disgusting!" He walked around the table and stood there crying as he looked at the doll. Abigail searched the room for a way to get Bill and her out of danger and saw the kitchen door.

Stan grabbed the doll and threw it against the wall. Abigail took a chance and jumped up and ran. Stan grabbed her and forced her back onto the chair.

"There's something I have to tell you." He sat next to her. "You see me and Mary Elizabeth we are together. We've been waiting for the perfect time to tell you."

"You're disgusting!" Abigail said.

"Disgusting? Let me tell you about my stomach turning each time I touched you."

It was quick. Stan had Abigail by her throat before she could say anything. Bill jumped up off the floor, he grabbed Stan by his arms and tried to shove him away but Stan knocked him back down to his knees and pointed the gun in his face. Stan turned his attention to Abigail.

"I can see you and your family are a problem," he sneered.

Abigail was quick as she jumped up and ran for the door. Stan was on her trail though, and when she reached the door handle, he snatched her by the throat. With one hand, he slammed her to the floor.

The grounds of Wood River Cemetery rumbled with whispers among the dead as the spirits left the boundaries of their afterlife.

*"It's Abigail,"* they said. *"She's in trouble."*

Abigail's seventh generation grandparents led the way and hovered over Margaret's house.

Inside Stan snatched Abigail up off the floor and shoved her toward the main hall. Bill got to his feet fast and rushed Stan. The impact landed both men out in the hall. Abigail ran back to the kitchen counter and grabbed a knife.

"You bastard," she said.

She knew if Stan left, if he killed her and Bill, he would get to Mary Elizabeth. At twenty-four, she was still a young woman. She has behaved much younger than her age. Her biggest blunder was Stan. But she was no coward. No one will harm her children. Her mother taught her that before she died.

"Let no one harm your child," her mother often chanted.

Like a witch's spell the words remained in Abigail's heart. Staring down at Stan's back, she raised that knife and let out a scream as she thrust downward. He turned on her fast, and forced her to let go of the knife and then kicked her in the chest. She fell backward and landed on her back. She saw Stan coming her way and turned onto her knees to crawl away from Stan.

"You filthy bitch," he said.

Abigail got to her feet and when she saw them, the ghosts of her great grandparents. She stumbled back.

"Oh, Oh, Oh," She said.

The woman ghost wore a bell shaped skirt and puffy sleeves. The man wore dark trousers and a jacket with a high collar. There were others, visible only to Abigail. She fell to her knees, her hands clasp to her chest.

Stan laughed at the sight. "I knew you were crazy," his tone demeaning. He raised the blade.

"Mary Elizabeth belongs to me!" he said.

*"Leave her be!"* the ghost said.

Stan flinched and dropped the knife to his side and stood there looking around, unable to move.

"Bill!" Abigail said. Bill came crawling to her. He reached her just in time to pull her out of the way. The ghost struck Stan and flew through him stopping on the other side. Abigail gasped at the harrowing look on Stan's face as she held Bill close. The ghosts pierced through Stan, one by one. His mouth fell open, eyes wide with fear, body jerking with each attack until he fell to the floor. When it was over Abigail nearly puked at the sight of Stan's mangled body.

# ELEVEN

"Jesus Bill! What the hell was that?" Abigail moved fast across the lawn.

"Abigail, wait," Bill said as he tried to keep up with her.

"Wait? I nearly pissed my pants back there!"

"Listen, I'll explain it to you. But right now we have two bodies back there." Bill grabbed Abigail's arm forcing her to the car. "Get in and go to Liz's. I'll be right behind you."

Both vehicles pulled out of the driveway as the ghosts faded away on the front lawn. Abigail saw them in her rearview mirror and shoved the gas pedal to the floorboard.

"I can't believe this shit," she said as she flew past the mailbox. She sped all the way to Liz's house.

Bill followed close behind her, though not as reckless. He arrived at Liz's where Abigail had just pulled in the driveway.

"You could have killed yourself driving that fast," Bill snapped.

"Oh like going after a crazed pedophile isn't dangerous," Abigail, snapped back. "You want to tell me what that was back there!"

"Look, I know it was risky. I shouldn't have gone there."

Abigail threw her arms up in the air, "I'm talking about the ghosts!"

Bill fumbled for words, and stumbled as he walked toward the door.

"Let's go inside, Liz and Margaret can tell you."

Abigail charged through the door. She took a couple of deep breaths, "Stan is dead."

Liz gawked at Bill.

He shook his head back and forth, "It wasn't me."

"No, it wasn't Bill! It was a bunch of damn ghosts! They were dressed like they were from the eighteen hundreds," Abigail said.

"I'll explain everything Abigail," Liz said. Then nodded over to Margaret.

Bill sat beside Margaret. "George?" He asked her and she shook her head. Tears welled in her eyes.

Bill put his arm around her. "You and George are my dearest friends. I'm here for you Margaret," he said.

Abigail said, "I, "Margaret, I'm sorry. I brought him here."

"It's not your fault, dear," Margaret said, though she found it difficult to breath. "Let's put the children to bed. Then we can talk about it."

"To bed, my children aren't getting out of my sight," Abigail said.

"You don't have to worry about the children. They're safe here," said Liz.

"Safe? Stan's dead, but let's not forget those ghosts back there." Abigail said.

"They're family, Abigail," Liz said. Margaret and Bill remained silent as Abigail's jaw dropped, mouth wide open.

"What, what do you mean family?"

"I'll explain what I can, Abigail. This all just came about, I assure you the children are safe. Let's get them to bed."

Liz and Abigail took the children upstairs.

Bill said, "George?"

"He was here. He's gone off somewhere."

"We have to call the police and report him missing," Bill said.

"Yes, yes I know."

"Can I get you something to drink Margaret?"

"Yes please. I'll have a cup of tea." She stood and walked slow to the kitchen. Bill said, "I'm impressed."

"About what?"

"You're holding yourself together well."

Margaret poured the hot water into her cup and sat on the stool. She wrapped her hands around the cup for warmth. Bill waited for her to respond half expecting a breakdown, and the other half, he didn't want to think of what the other half would do. With her psychic powers, he thought maybe she could bring hell to earth. She did neither. Bill watched her sit there looking worn but strong.

"Bill, there's trouble ahead." Margaret said.

"It's over now Margaret. Stan is dead."

"It's Alexandra, Bill. She's in trouble."

"How do you know Margaret?"

"She hasn't returned. Even when Stan went after Abigail, she didn't come."

"Wait, Margaret. How do you know Stan went after Abigail?"

"George."

Liz and Abigail came down stairs. Bill and Margaret watched them go into the home office.

"I guess it's time to tell Abigail about the family secret," Bill said. He grinned and then helped Margaret off the stool. They fell in behind Liz and Abigail in the office.

"Abigail, I painted this family tree, our family tree right after I moved into the house. It is through this tree they return."

Liz went on to tell the family history while calling out the names of those who had appeared. "There are many more," she said.

Margaret stood in the background listening to Liz. Bill moved to his right and when he did Margaret saw the tree and all the names. Alexandra's branch remained different from all the others. Liz continued to talk about the family, as Margaret stood quiet and worried, of what was to come.

***

In the other world, that of Alexandra's, Dalton stood over his wife mourning.

*"My Alexandra,"* he said. *"Come, dear, come back to me."*

Alexandra lay motionless. Sarah appeared before him and he took one look at her and knew she had not found who held his wife in the darkness. Whispers among the dead traveled across the earth's land where humans could only hear it as the wind. As the gusts grew stronger, the living took cover in their homes. The whine of the wind sounded like a human cry. It was Dalton's cry.

*"I'll find who holds you Alexandra,"* Dalton said.

The grounds shook. Liz leaned against the wall. Abigail grabbed the lamp and Bill grabbed Margaret and held her close until he looked at her face. Her mouth was wide open. Her head leaned back as she stared at the ceiling.

"Margaret!" Bill said.

"Oh dear Margaret," Liz said and moved to her side. She helped Bill get her out onto the sofa. "Margaret, dear friend, please tell me what's wrong." Bill's eyes watered and Liz saw him for the first time in his most vulnerable state. He had just lost his best friend and it seemed to age him.

Liz reached for Bill's face, her hands held him as his tears dribbled across her fingers. He went to turn away, but Liz's embrace, the emotional hold she had on him was strong, her hands were gentle, and her silence steadied him.

Margaret let out a scream. Her body rose off the sofa and thrashed across the room. Her limbs dangled helplessly midair against the wall.

Bill said "No!"

He rushed across the room. When he reached for Margaret, a crippling pain struck him and he rose several inches above the floor.

Abigail said, "I'm going to get my kids!"

Liz watched her dearest friends suffer until she couldn't bare it anymore.

"Who are you?" she said. "Show yourself!"

The flowers in the vase died off. Spider webs grew everywhere. The walls seeped a thick black substance. The air was smothering, every breath difficult.

"Show yourself!" Liz said.

It appeared by the stairs, sneered at her and then moved toward the top. Liz watched in horror at his wicked stare until it dawned on her. The children, it's going for the children!

"Abigail! Run!"

Liz ran toward the stairs. The evil entity threw her back and she tumbled across the floor.

Abigail grabbed both children. With Clara in her arms and Mary Elizabeth by her side she ran for the bedroom door. Then she saw it.

Mary Elizabeth saw it too and said, "Mommy," as she clung to her mother's leg. They stepped back a few feet. The evil presence blocked the doorway.

Abigail said, "Liz!"

Liz ran up the stairs. "Abigail!" Her voice trembled. She reached the doorway. She could see Abigail and the children straight through the ghost. "Whoever you are, you leave them alone!" With her arms open she plunged into it. It swirled and jerked her body. Liz had had enough. She let out a roar. Abigail stood watching them afraid to let go of her children.

"Leave her be!" said Abigail.

It stopped moving and threw Liz right out of its sphere sending her across the room.

Mary Elizabeth whimpered, "He's bad Mommy," she said.

"Who are you? What do you want?" Abigail said.

The mass hovered above the threshold, a disgusting puddle of thick black substance at its base swirled upward and into its mouth and out of its eyes. The liquid never leaving its host moved closer to Abigail and the children. Abigail covered Mary Elizabeth's eyes.

Liz pulled herself together and got to her feet. She saw the thing going for Abigail and the children. She ran full force toward the entity. The crazed looking spirit revealed its face as it threw its head back and let out an alarming shriek. Just as Liz reached it, just as she met the threshold it disappeared. Liz fell through the doorway and landed out in the hall.

"Liz!" Bill scrambled to get up the stairs. He reached the top and saw Liz on the floor.

"Liz, Liz, are you all right?"

Liz looked for Abigail and the children. "Where are they?"

She searched. "Oh no, oh no," she clung to Bill and pushed him away. She pulled at him again.

"Bill," she said.

She felt sick. She was about to throw up when she saw Abigail and the children peek through the doorway. "Oh dear God!" Liz said as she ran to them.

"Aunt Liz," Abigail said. "Who, what was that?"

"I don't know sweetie. I don't know," Liz said as she hugged her.

"He was the bad man Aunt Liz," Mary Elizabeth's voice sounded sweet. Liz picked her up and held her tight.

"He's after Alexandra." Margaret said. Her voice was monotone.

They turned and saw her at the top of the stairs. Her clothing dangled from her shoulders. It was impossible to think she had lost so much weight. Her hair fell out of its bun leaving her thick strands hanging around her frail looking shoulders.

"Mommy, is she hurt?" Mary Elizabeth asked.

"She's going to be ok," Abigail said.

"Margaret, who is he and why is he after Alexandra?" Liz said.

"Liz you have to return to the tree. You have to research their history." Margaret nearly fell backwards. Bill rushed to grab her before she tumbled down the stairs. Margaret raised her hand, stopping Bill. She needed to say it. "Alexandra is in trouble, they're all by her side."

"Who are they Margaret?" said Liz.

"Your ancestors Liz, your family, they are with her." Margaret nearly fell again.

"Come on, old gal. I need to get you to bed." Bill carried her to a guest room and got her into bed. He tucked her in and kissed her forehead.

"Margaret. Please tell me. What do I look for, I don't know where to find the information." Liz said.

"Use your research skills Liz. Find out who harmed Alexandra when she was alive." Margaret closed her eyes and was soon fast asleep.

# TWELVE

She's off. Way off. None of the records came together. She continued to search, determined to find more information on the lives of Alexandra and Dalton Ward.

"Margaret said a tragedy," Liz said aloud as she stared at her online tree. Abigail and Bill were in the other room entertaining the children. Margaret remained upstairs mourning. It was early yet and the skies were clear once again. The storm landed south of them and damage was minimal. Liz examined her facts and looked back at the tree.

"That's it!" She jumped up and gathered a notebook, pen, and her car keys. "Bill, Abigail!" She turned to exit the room and ran right into Bill.

"Going somewhere?" Bill grinned.

"Yes," she grinned herself. "I have to go into town, City Hall and the Library. There are some things I need to research. I'll call later." She flew past Abigail and the children.

Abigail looked at Bill and shrugged her shoulders.

"Bye Aunt Liz," said Mary Elizabeth.

"I have some things to do too," Bill said as he nodded toward the children. "Margaret and I have some chores to do," he said to Abigail.

Abigail shook her head and said, "… We'll stay here. I'll prepare dinner for later."

"It's ok Mommy." Mary Elizabeth said. Abigail kneeled down beside her and took her face in her hands.

"You'll help Mommy, won't you?"

Mary Elizabeth smiled, "Yes Mommy," she said.

"Good then," Bill said. He went upstairs leaving Abigail and the girls in the main room. Abigail eased over to the home office and pulled the door shut. Mary Elizabeth giggled.

"Just in case," Abigail said and smiled at her.

Mary Elizabeth giggled more.

"We'll be back soon," announced Bill. Abigail turned to see Bill and Margaret standing at the base of the stairs. She felt her own mouth drop. Margaret's hair looked mangled, her eyes distant and sad.

"Ok, we'll see you when you get back," Abigail said in her best cheerful voice.

*How lame Abigail.* She thought.

Margaret was quiet on the ride home. She looked over at Bill.

"I should have known," she said.

"Should have known what?"

"That it was George's time."

"Margaret, how could you have known?"

"He could see them Bill. He never saw them before," Margaret inhaled and exhaled. They were nearing the house. "Bill, please stop, I can't." Breathing was more difficult.

Bill pulled the truck to the side of the road. Margaret's home was off to the left, but the old farmhouse didn't feel like home without George.

"I can't go in there Bill."

"You stay in the truck. I will handle everything. I'll call the police from the kitchen," he said.

Margaret kept her head down and stared at her lap. She nodded. Bill pulled the truck up to the house and jumped out. He walked fast across the lawn. The front door was still open. He stepped across the threshold and saw George's body in the hall. He walked heavy-footed past him, entered the kitchen and rushed to the phone.

Margaret sat in the truck, her head down. A stream of tears fell onto her hands, she had clasped together on her lap.

*"Margaret"*

She heard him call her name. It sounded far away.

*"Margaret"*

She raised her head and there stood George out on the lawn. She turned her head away.

*"Margaret"*

Again, he called her name and he was close.

*"I am here"*

"Yes," she whispered, and looked to her left. He sat beside her on the driver's seat.

*"There is danger ahead."*

Margaret tightened her lips and squeezed her eyes shut. Her shoulders frail; her cheeks soaked. She nodded her head, yes, and nodded again, yes… yes… yes. She lifted her head, straightened her shoulders, and stepped out of the truck.

Bill continued to face the wall after he called 911.

"I'm sorry George," he said.

He banged his head three times on the wall, gathering the strength to continue. He turned around then fell back onto the wall. He clenched his chest and leaned forward gasping.

"Margaret, old gal," he caught his breath. "Try not to sneak up behind me like that."

George stood next to Margaret with a wide grin on his face.

"We will have to feed the animals and clean up before we return to Liz's house," Margaret said. Bill watched her move deliberately, but slowly across the room.

The brakes of the cruiser squealed, flashing lights appeared through the window. Margaret walked to the door and took hold of the knob. She looked over at Bill and then swung it open.

"Liz will need us later," she said.

\*\*\*

The library was less than four miles from Bill and Margaret. Liz sat in a corner scrolling through the old newspapers.

"Margaret said a tragedy," she said. She looked down at the paper in her hand, at the date again, November 1885. She looked back at the screen.

"The third," she whispered. She scrolled. She stopped.
*Boy Found Dead*

She leaned forward and read. *The body of young Eddie Ward, son of Mr. and Mrs. Dalton Ward found by the river.*

"Young Eddie was murdered," she gasped.

She scrolled through all the articles for that day and found nothing more.

"That's it? There must be more."

She scrolled to the next day, surely there would be more, she told herself. She kept scrolling. She found the obituary November 6… *laid to rest at Wood River Cemetery,* she read.

"A tragedy," she said. "Margaret said a tragedy." She scrolled.
*Man Murdered his Son's Killer*

She dropped her pen, bent over to pick it up, and smacked her forehead on the counter top. "Dammit."

She read. Right after the funeral Dalton found the man who raped and killed young Eddie. Witnesses said Dalton, crazed at the time, rushed toward Wilbur Savage. The encounter ended with Savage dead from a knife wound. Authorities arrested Dalton and later released him to the state hospital, the insane asylum.

Liz leaned back in the chair.

"Wilbur Savage," she said.

Sarah was there, suspended in the corner, watching Liz. Her sphere lucent and throbbing, she tried to leave. She thrashed about smacking the walls and ceiling.

She said, *"Brother-in-law!"*

Dalton heard her screams throughout the afterlife. He left his wife's side and traveled through dimensions to reach her until he appeared behind Liz. His sister-in-law, Sarah perched high in the corner of the room with her limbs stretched out clinging to the walls.

Liz pulled her sweater across her shoulders and folded her arms across her chest as she stared at the screen.

Dalton saw over her shoulder Wilbur Savage's name piercing through the screen at him.

Sarah's orb thrashed against the walls. She saw Dalton's face twisted and his eyes… his eyes crazed. She only saw him look like that once before, when he killed Wilbur Savage. She slammed into the wall one last time and broke through fleeing from his rage.

The building shook. Liz grabbed the counter. Books fell everywhere. She covered her head.

"Help me!"

She looked up at the ceiling and at the walls.

She yelled again, "Help!"

Dalton spun until his orb shriveled and completely disappeared. Then it was all calm. Liz peaked through her arms and saw it was clear. She raised her head and looked at the screen. It was blank. She stood and turned around to see a group of people staring at her.

A librarian asked, "Are you all right?"

Liz glanced around the room and saw the books were on shelves stacked in order; the room silent, except all eyes were on her.

"Yes. I… I must have had a seizure or something."

She gathered her things and walked past the glaring eyes. She managed a grin and nodded her head, avoiding eye contact and when she reached the door, she simply said, "Thank you."

She fumbled her way to her Honda, pulled her keys out of her bag, and looked back at the building. At first sight she saw the people inside were still watching her from the windows. She fell against her car and reached for the door handle. She tried to open the door.

Pulling on the handle, she said "Damnit, open."

She shoved the key in, turned the lock and jumped in the seat. She saw them again, staring from the windows as she turned the ignition. Too many dead faces to count, all harrowing eyes on her. She turned the corner, wheels screeching, over in the tree line another one, eyes on Liz. She slammed on the brake and held onto the steering wheel tight as the car spun out of her control until it crashed against a tree. Blood dripped over her brow. She opened her eyes and peered out of the windshield.

"I know you're there," she said as she searched for their eyes.

She saw the headlights of an oncoming car through the trees. Dusk had just fallen, had she got there sooner she would not be seeing the fast moving vehicle.

"Oh no Lizzie you're in the wrong lane!"

She stepped on the gas, wheels spinning; she saw the car near, moving fast.

"Come On!"

Her rear wheel grabbed the pavement and she shot across the black top nearly crashing into another tree as the other car screeched and sped east. She straightened out onto the roadway, her thoughts reeling as she drove away.

She made it home and slammed the door against the wall. Abigail stood before her holding a bowl in her hands.

Liz looked over at the office door, "Who closed the door!"

She ran over, opened the door, and turned to see Abigail and the children. Their expressions dumbfounded. Liz searched the room.

"Where's Bill?"

Abigail stuttered, "He, he…"

"Where's Bill!"

"Liz! He went with Margaret to her place. What is wrong with you? You're scaring the kids!"

Liz exhaled. Abigail watched her hand shake as she reached her forehead. The blood still wet and smeared.

Liz looked at her fingers and then back to Abigail.

"Liz, what happened?"

"He was murdered," she said.

"Murdered," Abigail said, "Who was murdered, where?"

"Eddie, he was seven years old. He was raped and killed!"

"Liz that's horrible! Do his parents know?"

Liz snapped, "Of course they know! He killed Wilbur Savage!"

"Who killed him?" Abigail asked.

"Dalton, who else would I be talking about, your ancestors!"

Mary Elizabeth pulled on Abigail's sweater, "Wilbur Mommy, the bad man," Mary Elizabeth said.

Abigail kneeled beside her, and touched her hair; she then stood and faced Liz.

She threw her hands up in the air.

"She's barely four years old, and she knows what you're talking about, who the hell is Wilbur Savage!"

Glasses chattered and the lights flickered. Abigail steadied herself.

"What was that?" she asked Liz. She picked Clara up and said, "Mary Elizabeth stay with Mommy."

They gathered in the center of the room. Liz spun around and looked down at Mary Elizabeth, "Sweetie, she said, "How do you know Wilbur?"

# THIRTEEN

"Margaret," Bill said. "George was a good man."

"Is a good man," Margaret said. He glanced over at her, keeping the truck on the road. Her face stern yet relaxed.

She nodded her head and said, "He's in the back."

Bill turned the wheel to the left, tires spun on the damp soil until he was back on the road again.

"Margaret," Bill peered through his rearview mirror, "George," he said. "You two... I don't know how I would have handled the loneliness if it weren't for the two of you. You know after Stephanie died. I mean it when I say you're my dearest friends."

"She says to tell you, it's ok." Margaret's motherly voice was calm.

Bill hit the brakes. The tires screeched to a halt. He sat there stalled in the middle of the road. He gripped the steering wheel and stared at Margaret.

"She's here?"

"She's been here all along Bill."

"But, why hasn't she... I haven't seen her, why?"

"You weren't ready."

"I've been ready since the day she died."

"She says you never cried Bill." Her voice calm and soft.

"I wasn't ready for her to die!"

"She says she had to go, Bill."

Bill teared, "I stayed with her till the end."

"Yes, you did Bill."

"She was beautiful." He leaned his head forward, his grip stronger on the wheel, "I want her to know that."

"She says you're ready Bill."

Bill raised his head, "Where is she?"

"She's close. She says it's ok Bill."

"What's OK?"

Margaret said, "You and Liz. She says it's ok."

He raised his head. Margaret saw his pain, his surprise at her comment, and the love in his eyes when he saw the ghost of his wife outside the window. He couldn't do anything but stare at her, his cries admirable, until she faded away.

"Bill," Margaret said. "You're a good man."

He wiped his face with his sleeve, but the tears kept falling as he threw the truck in gear. He said, "Margaret, old gal, I do my best."

"I think we should get back to Liz," Margaret said.

They were quiet as Bill drove to Liz's house. He pulled into Liz's driveway.

"The lights are out," he said.

He got out of the truck and leaned forward and listened through the door for any noise on the other side. He raised his hand to grab the door handle, but stopped and took a deep breath.

He said, "What if they're hurt?"

Margaret took his arm in hers and said with a calm tone, "Bill we have to go inside the house."

He grabbed the handle and turned the knob. He pushed the door open and peeked inside the dark space.

"The fire's still glowing," he said. "They must be asleep by the fire."

Bill inched his way toward the flickering flames with Margaret on his heels. He kept his eyes on the floor thinking, they could all be dead. Margaret felt his hesitancy. She shoved him to the side, and rushed toward the living room.

"They aren't in here," she said.

Bill pushed past Margaret and said, "Her car is in the garage. They must be here."

He ran up the stairs yelling, "Liz, Abigail!"

He couldn't imagine where they were, and thought perhaps they were out walking, "No, no, that doesn't make sense," he said as he descended the stairs.

"Margaret, do you see them?" He stopped when he saw Margaret in the same spot she was before he went upstairs, her expression somber and omniscient.

"Margaret what is it?"

"The cellar, we should look in the cellar."

"The cellar," he said as he zipped past her heading for the basement. He prayed Liz was safe. He reached the cellar door.

"Liz!"

The galvanized steel built to protect now stood as a barrier between him and Liz. He pounded the door yelling for Liz until he heard the clank of the lock and then the squeal of the hinges. He pulled the door open and there stood Abigail with Clara in her arms.

"Thank goodness," he said.

"Bill!" Mary Elizabeth said looking up at Bill.

He took her face in his palms.

"I'm so happy to see you," he said and then stepped further into the space relieved they were all right.

"Liz, I...."

The lamp in the corner did little to light the room, water and canned goods lined up on the far wall, two cots and a stack of blankets over to the right, no sign of Liz. He stared into the room, "Where is she?"

"I don't know."

He turned to her, "Abigail, where is she?"

"I don't know Bill! She just disappeared!"

"Disappeared?" Abigail people don't just disappear! Where did you leave her!" he yelled. Until he saw, Abigail's lips tremble.

"I'm sorry," he said. "Please tell me, Abigail, what happened to Liz."

"The bad man took her," Mary Elizabeth's teary brown eyes focused on Bill.

"Mary Elizabeth," he said. "What bad man?"

"Wilbur Savage," she said.

"Do you know where they went?"

Margaret stood about four feet away, her voice weary as she channeled her energy, "She's on the other side," she said.

***

Liz struggled to open her eyes. Dampness against her cheek felt like flesh, of human or animal she did not know. The rancid smell burned her nostrils. She choked and tried to lift her head but dropped it back down and felt something cold and slimy slither under her cheek. Repulsed and stricken she raised her body and crawled until she reached a wall. Her back pressed against its jagged edge. A trickle of something liquid followed by a burble caused her to open her eyes. It was black, slimy and thick. It seethed from the wall. All though no one appeared before her, she felt its presence and heard its hiss next to her and across the room.

"Show yourself!"

It moved close and hissed loud in her ear. She cringed and rushed away. The voices were all around her, whispers, and screams.

"*They can't help you,*" they said.

"*Save her,*" another said.

Liz was dizzy and nauseous. She saw something glow in the distance.

As she crept in its direction she thought of Abigail and the children. They were horrified when it entered the house.

She told them, "Go! Run to the cellar!"

Maybe if she had run with them she wouldn't be alone in this surreal chamber of darkness.

Maybe it was meant to be, all the lonely nights, the creepy sounds and visions, maybe it lead to this all along, her end.

The air was thick, she tasted its bitter mist, and it reeked of death. Each step she took, deliberate, careful not to trip on the uneven rock beneath her shaky legs. Norwich she thought, it's the same as the sidewalks of Norwich. The walls pressed down on her and shut her in as she searched for an escape.

As she stood in the darkness at the edge of the glowing sphere, she saw a bed raised from the ground. Old decrepit roots of a tree reached from its base to the top intertwined to form the shape of a body. From it, the black slimy liquid seeped through the spaces between the branches and across a human hand protruding from its cage. The slithering sound of the muck squeezing through narrow passages caused Liz to gasp, as it appeared to inhale and exhale it revealed the face of a woman.

Clinching her own chest, Liz thought back to the menacing threats of storms, and the whispers around the house, had it all lead to this, the yearning for family, her passion for ancestry, and her painted tree.

The face of the woman tied down by wicked twine turned toward Liz. A rush of realization swarmed Liz as she peered through the mist.

"Alexandra?"

Liz dropped her mouth open. The foul taste of rotted remains, and gases filled her throat. She coughed and tried to speak again. The sound of her voice, lost.

*Help her.*

She felt the touch of cold flesh on her shoulder. Its fingers were long and shriveled, with pointed filthy nails. It raised its hand, pointed the index, and tapped on her shoulder. On the third tap, Liz cowered to the ground on her hands and knees and clawed away from the beast. She searched for a place to hide.

*Stop, stop, stop it Liz!*

She pounded her fist on the ground.

"You will not take me!"

It moved across the eerie room, its laugh malicious and arrogant.

Liz stood on her feet and faced him.

"Who are you!" she said.

Whispers echoed all around her, many voices, one after the other, some sounded far away and others close. They repeated the same name.

"Wilbur Savage, Wilbur Savage... WILBUR SAVAGE!"

Liz took a quick breath and looked over at Alexandra.

It dawned on her; he can't go in the sphere.

He held Alexandra captive with his wicked roots, but her sphere protected her. She braced herself with a couple of deep breaths.

"Screw you Wilbur Savage!" she yelled, and stepped inside the sphere.

Wilbur Savage said, "No!"

Liz fell to the ground. Wilbur shifted from demon to a human and back. Liz got to her feet and ran to Alexandra.

She said, "Alexandra!"

Alexandra awakened with a banshee's wail!

Liz grabbed the branches, and ripped the slick strands away from her great grandmother.

The shrivel tone of his voice, deceptive and eerie, "I see," Wilbur's words echoed throughout the massive chamber. As if defeated, he faded into the darkness.

As he went, his last words "Tell me… Liz, how is young Mary Elizabeth.

# FOURTEEN

"She's gone to the other side." Margaret said it again.

Bill put his arm around Mary Elizabeth and held her tight.

"She's in the afterlife," Margaret's tone was serious as she used her clairvoyant gift to find Liz.

"Wait, you can see her?" Abigail said as she held Clara's head to her chest.

Margaret turned around to face the stairs behind them, her head down as she searched the afterlife.

"She's with Alexandra," she said, as she took the first step up the stairs. Bill, Abigail and the children followed her to the living room.

Abigail bundled the children in front of the fireplace and touched their faces as they drifted off to sleep. She gazed over to Margaret who sat close by, in what seemed a trance.

"Anything?" Bill asked.

"No. Bill, do you think she can bring Liz back."

Bill reached over to her and touched her shoulder he said, "We'll see, Abigail."

He knew Liz was on the other side, dead, and she wasn't coming back, at least not in the life form Abigail's holding on to, not as the living. He couldn't say the words. Instead, he chose to let Abigail see for herself when Liz returns in her new form, a ghostly shadow of the woman they both love. Looking over at the two girls lying on the floor, he knew his new role. He would be like family to them and to Abigail, who sat beside him appearing lost as she sipped coffee.

Bill said, "Stan?"

"What about him?"

"Why him?"

"I don't know," she said. "There wasn't anyone else at the time. He was good with Mary Elizabeth," Abigail fumbled the words. "Well, you know what I mean." She shifted in her seat and put her mug on the coffee table. Bill watched her as she swept the hair away from her eyes. An amazing likeness of Liz, high cheekbones set on a perfect oval face. Her mouth quivered as she leaned her forehead onto her palm, tears flowed down her arms.

"I brought that man in my home, around my daughter."

"You didn't know he would hurt Mary Elizabeth. You are not to blame Abigail," Bill said.

Sarah's apparition appeared and kneeled beside Abigail. She remembered her pain when Wilbur killed her nephew. She couldn't face anyone, even her sister. Dalton spent years telling her she wasn't to blame, yet, she chose to close herself inside her home and live her days alone. She now looked at Abigail's frailness and worried guilt would wear on her as it did to her when she lived.

*"I must find Alexandra,"* she said as she moved away from Abigail and returned to the afterlife.

Abigail felt a breeze and reached for Liz's throw.

"Are you cold?" Bill asked.

"Just a chill," Abigail said as she pulled the cover around her shoulders.

"I couldn't manage alone Bill. My phone was disconnected. I was behind on my electric. Stan came along and bought the house. He took care of all the bills." Her mouth quivered, "I should have seen. Bill, he isolated me from others. He wouldn't put a phone in the house. All the signs were there. This is my fault, everything that's happened."

Across the room Margaret said, "It's coming."

"What is it?" Abigail leaned forward and looked over at her girls.

Bill sat his cup down and moved to the edge of his seat. Whatever was on the way it wasn't Liz and by the tone of Margaret's voice it had to be trouble.

"Get the girls," he said.

Abigail sprung into action catching her leg between the sofa and coffee table and stumbled toward the girls.

"What is it Bill?" she said.

Bill raised his hand to hush her.

The fire crackled as soft glows of light flickered across the room. Abigail searched focusing on the bright areas, but the darkness drew her in as she tried to see movement.

"Is something here?" she whispered.

Bill hushed her again as he listened. Snakes he thought, it sounded like snakes slithering in the corners. They sounded wet. He had a hunch to pick his feet up off the floor, as if he were about to be snatched and dragged away. He felt the slick movement across his shoe as he squeezed his thighs and then fixed his eyes on Abigail.

"Bill?" Abigail saw his pale face. The sweat above his upper lip shimmered in the fire's light. Her girls looked angelic in her arms. Her grip tightened across their small bodies as she managed to keep from screaming. A slapping noise to her right startled her. She raised the girls higher up her chest. She heard another slapping noise to her left. Her feet, she thought about her feet and then she felt something move across them.

"No." She told herself.

The slaps continued to smack against a wet surface as she squeezed her eyes shut. Slimy snake like creatures covered her in an instant. Her nostrils burned from the stench, and she heard them everywhere.

"Let no one harm my girls," she said. "Let no one harm my girls."

In an instant they were gone. She opened her eyes a saw Bill staring at her.

"It is over," she said.

She hugged both girls simultaneously thankful it ended. Bill's expression was grave as she caught his stare; he dropped his eyes down toward her chest. Abigail followed his path and in her arms a dark stump of a tree whittled away where Mary Elizabeth had been.

"W... Where is she?" Abigail said. She looked at Clara, who rested in her arms. "I held her! I didn't let go!"

Margaret sat up, back straight, eyes wide, she said, "He took her!"

"W... Who?" Abigail said.

Bill stood up tall, his jaw clenched, "Wilbur Savage," he said.

Abigail got to her feet, Clara on her hip, and balled her fist swinging aimlessly into the air, "Please Margaret, do something,".

Bill paced with a short gait and before Margaret could answer Abigail he said, "We will get her back!"

Abigail hung her hand to her side. Her voice cracked, she said, "No Bill." Her knees weakened as she barely made it to the sofa without collapsing. "No," she repeated.

Bill rushed to her side, "Abigail, listen to me," he held her face refusing to let her look away. "We will get her back. Listen, he's only trying to scare us." Bill looked over at Margaret, "Isn't that right. Tell her Margaret." He looked back at Abigail, "You listen to me. I will get her back."

"She's my responsibility," Abigail said. She kept her gaze on Clara's face and fell silent.

"Margaret, tell me what to do," Bill snapped.

"We wait," she said.

Bill darted across the room, an urgent whisper, "We can't wait, we can't," he paused and tugged at her arms. "Is there something you can do Margaret?"

"She's on the other side. We cannot reach her."

"On the other side? What the hell does that mean! Are you saying she's dead too?" Bill's voice quivered. He looked over at Abigail.

"Not dead." Margaret said.

Bill whipped his head toward Margaret, "She's not dead. Ok, ok, how do we get her back?" He grabbed her thighs and held tight. "I'll go there Margaret. I will. Show me, show me how."

Margaret leaned forward and gradually stood. Bill rose from his kneeled position and watched her closely.

"Her physical body remains here," she said.

Abigail rose to her feet, "She's here?"

"Her body is here, but her spirit is with him."

Bill paced across the floor. "We find her body and then you send me to the other side." He ran his hands through his hair. He stuttered, "This could work, right?"

He and Abigail met each other's eyes. They both bolted into action. "Here, hold her," Abigail threw Clara in Margaret's arms. They searched each room.

"Anything?" Bill said as they met in the hall upstairs.

"No." Abigail's voice, determined. Liz's bedroom was the only room left. Each knew if Mary Elizabeth wasn't in there… they couldn't think about it. Together they sprinted toward the door and pushed it open. Abigail's grip on the door handle kept her from falling to her knees. There on Liz's bed lay Mary Elizabeth unharmed.

Bill's mouth shut before he could form the words. He staggered forward; his lips parted again, he said, "Liz."

Abigail reached the bedside first and stood with her hand over her mouth. Bill stepped behind her. He said, "They're both here." They heard a whimper behind them and turned to see Margaret standing in the doorway with Clara

"She's fussy," she said. Clara leaned her head back on Margaret's chest.

Bill said, "Margaret, old gal, they're both here."

"I see," Margaret stayed in the doorway.

"Margaret," Bill said, "Does this mean Liz is alive too?"

"Yes, it does Bill, but she may not know it."

Abigail paced just once and returned to the bedside she said, "I'll go there. Just send me. I'll bring them back."

Margaret stepped into the room. Her voice cracked, "I'm afraid it's not that easy."

Bill said, "I'm afraid it's not that easy? Margaret surely there's something we can do. We understand it's not easy but can we do it?"

"Someone from the other side has to take you there."

"So we'll find someone, right Bill?" Abigail said. She looked him straight in the eye. He felt her unwavering stare. Right then he understood the depth of their relationship, their bond to each other and to the cause. He gazed at Liz. The thought of her lost on the other side believing she's dead. She'll never try to come back if she thinks she's dead.

He looked away and back at Abigail's glare, "Abigail, call upon your dead ancestors. Get them to take you there."

"How? I don't know how to 'call upon' them," she said.

They both paused and then at the same time they looked at Margaret.

# FIFTEEN

Liz stood facing her. She's taller than she imagined. Her long hair tangled, eyes bewildered. "Alexandra," Liz said.

Alexandra stared wide-eyed. It was as if she didn't recognize her.

"Grandmother?" Liz said as she took a half step back.

Alexandra flew up toward the ceiling and then circled the room. By the time Liz caught up with her movement, she was back in front of her. Her long white dress fluttered around her as she paused and examined Liz.

"Alexandra," Liz repeated.

"Who brought you here?" Alexandra said.

Liz stumbled further back and stuttered, "Wilbur Savage."

Alexandra swayed sideways. She looked up to the ton of rock above them. A black substance dripped throughout the ominous room.

"Dalton!" she said.

Her voice echoed throughout the darkness.

Liz covered her ears and watched her search the area.

"Alexandra, Wilbur's gone after Mary Elizabeth! I need your help!" she said.

Alexandra rushed toward Liz, she said, "Where is Dalton?"

She spoke without moving her lips, telepathy, Liz thought as she said, "I don't know." She wondered if her own lips moved. She raised her hands to her ears, back muscles tight and she hunched over, waiting for another scream from Alexandra.

An eerie and threatening laugh came from the far corner. It silenced both Liz and Alexandra. It had to be Wilbur. Alexandra moved closer to Liz as they both stared into the darkness. Liz reached for her cold hand and welcomed her firm grip. Her flesh was soft and clammy with a rippled effect, like water waves traveling through her skin.

Wilbur said, "Hello Liz," in a menacing voice. His voice echoed throughout and correlated with the sound of the dripping black liquid that Liz understood to be his blood, as dead as he was. It caged them in trapping them, perhaps in the evil spirit himself.

"You are correct Liz," said Alexandra.

Alexandra's voice came from within her own head, *"Can you hear me?"* Liz asked without speaking the words outward.

"Yes."

Good, Liz thought as she examined the space. Branches protruded through the boulders. Each snap of a twig echoed as if the chamber was a small part of a much larger space. A light shimmered off each mangled arm. There had to be a way home.

"What's on the other side?" she asked Alexandra.

"The family."

"Our family? Can't you call them to help?"

The vile snicker from Wilbur resonated.

"Shut up! You bastard!" Liz said.

The tree branches above snapped in unison, each reaching further into the confined space.

"Interesting," he sneered. "You don't recognize your own family tree."

Liz couldn't see him, but his slithering tongue and devilish hiss heard from all angles of the barren space tore at her gut leaving her nauseous.

"How generous of you, painting that tree," his voice mocking.

Liz took short deep breaths and gritted her teeth, "Show yourself you coward."

Bile reached her throat. She tried holding it in but her stomach gurgled forcing the crude contents up to her mouth and out splattering across the ground. Nothing will stop her. She wiped her face with her bare hand and frowned when she saw it was still flesh. Something's amiss. She thought. Then, as if being face to face with a demon wasn't enough, she realized she wasn't a ghost. She spoke to Alexandra, "I'm not dead. Am I?"

Alexandra gazed upon Liz. She said, "You are alive."

"Then how am I here?"

Alexandra faced the dark corner from which Wilbur lurked.

"Why have you brought her here?" she asked with a stark tone.

His face appeared through the darkness, switching back and forth from man to demon, both revealing rage. "I want the truth told," he hissed.

"You killed my son!"

Liz stood back watching. She looked at her arms, flesh; she was no match against the dead. At least not physically. *Think, think,* she told herself. The sound of the tree branches cracking and slithering above grew louder, Liz looked up and saw they were growing into massive roots reaching further into the chamber.

*You don't recognize your own family tree.* She thought.

"That's it!" Liz yelled. She scanned the walls.

"Climb," she whispered.

It's crazy to think her hand-painted family tree rests above the wicked roots, but no crazier than her being alive in the underworld. The shimmers of light she saw from the pit had to be her lamp from her office. She hoped she was right as she ran to the wall.

The blood of the demon seeped from the roots that now reached the base of the chamber. Liz grabbed onto them climbing only a small ways before she slipped back onto the floor. Wilbur's blood smeared her hands and clothing.

"Alexandra!"

She grabbed another root and pulled herself up, her hands slid but she held tight and hoisted herself upward. Alexandra faced Wilbur Savage, staged as a barrier between him and her descendent.

Liz continued to grab onto anything she could inching her way up to her hand-painted tree. A voice from below echoed throughout the chamber. A child's voice, "Great Aunt Liz!"

Liz froze. "This can't be real," she told herself. She leaned her head against the wet surface, the rancid odor burned her throat, please, don't let this be.

Another cry, "Great Aunt Liz!"

Liz let go and slid down to the floor. Her face covered with the blood of a demon, one that now had her great niece, Mary Elizabeth. Of flesh or not she had no choice but to confront him.

"Let her go!"

The demon's face enlarged and closed in on Liz, "The truth!" he said.

Alexandra said, "Leave her be!" She and Liz side by side, Mary Elizabeth a few feet away covered with dead tree limbs, Wilbur's black blood oozing around her, her angel eyes wide and filled with tears.

Liz reached for Mary Elizabeth, the poignant tone of her own voice upsetting, she asked, "What truth?" She spoke again, only this time without speaking the words, she spoke to Alexandra.

"Grandmother, please help me save Mary Elizabeth, please."

"Call Dalton." Wilbur's shrewd demand chilled Liz.

Alexandra turned around to face him, "No!"

"Call him! Or I take the child!"

Liz couldn't bear to think what he would do to her. She wanted to scream, but held back, "Please, Grandmother call Dalton, call my Grandfather."

"It's a trap granddaughter."

Liz looked up at the ceiling. She was sure that if she made it to the top she'd return to her world, convinced that when she painted her family tree she unknowingly invited this demon in, and through her tree he had laid waiting to abduct her and now Mary Elizabeth. Piece by piece she put it together. How she got there, the way back, she kept glancing up at the ceiling, the truth, all she needed was the truth.

*What truth?*

The agonizing few seconds of silence tore at Liz's heart. "Just answer me, you Bastard!"

"Tell her Alexandra. Tell her about Dalton."

"I know not what you speak of," Alexandra said.

90

"Who is the last person you saw your son with before he went missing?"

Alexandra remembered the air was cool; rain was near their small Rhode Island town. She remembered all right the last time she saw her son alive, climbing into Dalton's wagon. His hazel eyes wide and sad as he looked back at her and waved his small hand goodbye. She remembered waving back to her only son. She waved at Dalton too, but he did not see, he never looked back. That was the last time she saw her son alive.

Alexandra buried that memory of Dalton long before she even died, that he never looked back. The scene replayed as she stood before Wilbur Savage. Her head shook back and forth, she whispered, "No."

Wilbur's insulting sneer, his allusion that Dalton, her loving husband had something to do with her son's disappearance infuriated her, but her thoughts raced back to the last day she saw her son alive.

"Dalton!"

Liz tried holding her stance, but the walls vibrated with each of Alexandra's screams, each growing more like a pathetic cry. Liz collapsed to the floor but kept her eyes on Mary Elizabeth.

"It's ok sweetie," she yelled to her.

The demon's black blood dripped from the ceiling and pooled onto the floor, thick and acrid. It swirled back up to the ceiling and back down again. More puddles formed until its evil trap surrounded its occupants.

Mary Elizabeth said, "Dalton's a bad man!"

"No!" Alexandra's spirit simultaneously faced forward and backward. Her face, a frozen grimace. "Hush, child! You know not what you speak of!"

She remembered all right the look in Dalton's eyes when he returned without her son.

"He ran off," he had said.

"Why Dalton, why did he run?" she had asked him.

He shifted his eyes downward, turned his head away from her, "We will find him, don't you worry."

He never explained why her son ran. And it was Dalton, who found their son dead down by the river. She heard his cry in the distance and ran, gulping her worst fear, to the site where her baby lay slain. She remembered now, the rage on Dalton's face when she found the necklace her sister made and gave to Wilbur Savage. It all came back to her in flashes.

"You brought that man into my home!" She had said to her only sister.

Dalton had shifted his eyes over to the tree line.

Alexandra moaned. The memory she had blocked during her life and in death threatened to crush her.

A flashback, over in the tree line Wilbur Savage stood with a wicked grin. She remembered how he mocked Dalton.

Alexandra whimpered as she moved away from Liz and Mary Elizabeth. Flashing face forward and backward until she stopped. Her back turned on them.

"Alexandra." Liz said. Alexandra remained quiet, her back turned.

"Grandmother?"

Liz looked over to Mary Elizabeth and at Alexandra and then back at Mary Elizabeth, tears drenched the child's cheeks as she stared at Alexandra.

"What is it? Mary Elizabeth."

Mary Elizabeth slumped her shoulders, her chin lowered. Liz could see the doom hovering over her.

"Alexandra, please help," she said.

Wilbur's evil tone was clear, "Bring Dalton to me or I take the child for my own," he hissed. He ran his long filthy fingernail over her cheek, he said, "This delicious angel."

"Leave her alone!" Liz said.

Liz remembered when her husband died. The whispers amongst her friends and the children, victims they said. She had to leave. She couldn't face them with the truth.

*The truth.*

She ran toward Alexandra, "Please tell me when you last saw your son?"

Alexandra remained quiet.

"You have to say it!"

"No!" Alexandra said. The room shook.

92

Liz looked up toward the ceiling. The ton of rock shifted and she saw more light between the boulders. She stumbled back but kept her gaze through the opening. There above them, she saw her office lamp. Abigail would be there. Liz's memories flooded her mind and sickened her gut. Abigail was a sweet child, quiet and careful. Liz loved her like a daughter. She remembered her husband slipping back into bed. She never talked about it and the only strength she had left, she used to shower Abigail with hugs and kisses. Brad, her pedophile husband, died. Rumors spread in the neighborhood; people whispered their ugly words. All of it true. Abigail was one of many. The thought pressed heavy on Liz's chest.

*I should have said something.*

She turned to see Mary Elizabeth.

# SIXTEEN

"Margaret, will it work?" Bill searched the room for the third time. "Abigail, you don't have to do this. I can go," he said.

Abigail placed her hand on Bill's forearm with a firm grip she said, "Bill, I have to be the one. I don't know why, I just feel it."

"Do you hear that?" Margaret asked.

The sound drew them to the home office. The voice of one person, a woman, "It sounds like someone calling my name," Abigail said.

Margaret led them as they entered the office. Empty.

"Let's see here," Margaret's intuition was usually right. She walked to the family tree and stood beside the lamp.

Bill and Abigail stood behind her peeking over her shoulder. "I don't see anything," Abigail said.

"Me either," said Bill.

"Quiet," said Margaret.

Bill and Abigail looked at each other and shrugged their shoulders.

"There," Margaret pointed her finger to the painting.

"I see names Margaret. That's all I see." Bill looked over to Abigail and shrugged his shoulder again.

"We'll have the séance right here," Margaret announced.

"Right here?" Bill asked, "Margaret, it's tight in here don't you think."

Margaret pointed to the tree.

"Liz and Mary, they are there."

Bill walked over to the wall and read the names. "What are you talking about Margaret?"

Abigail said, "I'll get the candles."

Bill scratched his head and watched Margaret turn the lamp off and then back on again.

"Excuse me Bill," Bill jump out of the way as Abigail placed lit candles around the room.

"There." Margaret pointed at the tree, "You'll go through there," she said to Abigail.

"Ok."

"Now, wait a minute. She'll go through where?" Bill studied Margaret's face thinking she can't be serious.

"The tree is the portal."

Margaret turned the lamp off and then turned it back on again.

"Margaret, why are you turning the light on and off?" Bill expected an answer, but Margaret just kept fooling with it. He didn't ask again, instead he made sure he was out of the way.

Abigail took her sweater off and waited for Margaret's instructions. Her eyes wide, half-wild looking as she prepared herself for the trip to the other side. She steadied her breathing and closed her eyes pausing for a moment to take a deep breath. She opened her eyes to see Bill's face only a few inches from hers.

"You don't have to do this Abigail."

"Bill, I'm going."

The light went out and on again.

"I'm worried," Bill said as he grabbed Abigail's shoulders. Darkness.

"Margaret dear, please leave the light alone!" Bill snapped.

"Listen," she said.

They stood in the darkness, listening. "I hear you two breathing, and that's about it," Bill said.

"Shush," Margaret cut him off as she kept her hand on the light switch. The call was faint and far away.

Bill stepped closer to the wall, "What is that?" he asked.

"It's a call for Abigail," said Margaret.

"Wait, is that Liz!" Bill placed his hands on the wall, and pressed in several spots as if looking for a secret passage.

"How do we get to her?"

He turned to see Margaret and Abigail, both giving him an odd look, "What?"

Abigail nodded over to the corner of the room. Bill shifted his eyes first without moving his head.

"Another ghost," he said.

The lamp flickered. "Margaret, please leave the lamp alone," Bill moaned.

"I'm not touching the lamp Bill," she said.

"He's doing it," said Abigail as she pointed to the ghost.

The lights went out. Bill grabbed Margaret and Abigail's hands. His hands were sweaty. *Oh God Bill, hold it together,* Abigail thought as he squeezed her hand.

In the corner, left of the hand painted tree his spirit levitated. His ghostly eyes peered at Abigail. She felt his stare bearing down on her, suffocating her. Doom lingered deep within the hazel eyes of Dalton's transparent face. A quiver fluttered across her stomach as she stood there staring back at him. She had seen it before, that look of guilt. She replayed the past in her mind. She was ten years old. Her Aunt Liz didn't hear Brad as he slipped out of their bedroom. She didn't hear his moans as he laid on top of her either. The next morning and every morning after he violated her he had that same look on his face. The same expression Dalton had now, guilt and pity on me bullshit she endured many years ago.

"No," she said aloud as she back away.

"Oh my God," Abigail said as she freed her hands from Margaret's tight grip. "I have to get to Liz."

"Join hands, we'll summon Sarah," Margaret said.

"We're cursed. Just like Mom said all those years." Abigail repeated as she held hands with Bill and Margaret in the candle lit room. She closed her eyes, repeated her words. She thought of Brad and Stan, her throat dried. Guilt swelled inside her. She had to get to Liz and tell her the truth, that she never stopped Brad, she never told either. If she had, he would not have claimed all those victims, innocent children whose memories surely haunt them today as adults. Saliva formed in her mouth as the urge to puke struck with her next thought... she saw the same look on Stan's face. He claimed her daughter and it was right in front of her. The signs were there and she blocked them, she had buried them deep inside and wished, even today, that none of it ever happened.

Screw it, she said to herself. Her daughter is on the other side suffering God only knows what, at the hands of Wilbur Savage! Her chant grew louder and louder until the ghost of Sarah appeared with her arms stretched out, reaching for her. Abigail caught her breath as she stared into her ghostly eyes, her dark brown expressive eyes. If she didn't know better she'd think she looked into the eyes of her own daughter, Mary Elizabeth, but as an adult. She was captivated and without forethought, she grabbed Sarah's hands. Instantly the room seemed to disappear as Abigail allowed Sarah to take her to the other side.

"Did they go in there?" Bill asked, pointing at the family tree.

"I suspect they did," said Margaret.

"What do we do?" Bill paced a couple of quick steps.

"We wait."

Bill took a couple more quick steps and walked right out of the office. Margaret remained quiet as Bill let it all sink in. She knew he'd walk back in the room.

Bill stuck his head in and peered around the doorframe, "What are we waiting for, exactly."

"Good question Bill. I suspect Liz and her family has been subject to a curse."

"Margaret, how do you figure?"

"I've been thinking about it. I believe it all started in 1885, maybe further back in time. Liz's ancestor, Young Eddie she called him. He was murdered, raped and left by the river to die. Young Eddie's father, Dalton killed Wilbur Savage before police could take him in custody."

"Yeah, so," Bill said as he walked Margaret into the living room.

"The only witness to the crime and the victim was dead."

"So, what are you saying Margaret?"

"Fast forward, if you will, Bill. Remember the serial killer that died here in this house?"

"You're speaking about Randy Sullivan, yes, what about him?"

"There was a piece in the newspaper about his life. It told of his youth and his abusive father. A victim of incest you see."

"What's that have to do with Liz and her family?"

"Stan was after Mary Elizabeth."

"I'm not catching on to what you're trying to tell me Margaret."

"I suspect Abigail has a secret too."

Bill's mind raced. He ran his hand through his hair, "What secret?"

"I think Liz's husband, Brad harmed her."

"You mean," he stuttered. "Liz knows about it?"

"No Bill, I don't think she knows. That's why Abigail has gone to the other side, to tell her."

"Wait," Bill leaned forward and placed his hand on the coffee table pointing with his index finger as if he'd found something right there on that spot. "You're telling me they are cursed with incest, rape and murder?"

Margaret nodded her head in agreement.

"Why, I mean, Margaret what does this mean?"

Margaret rested her back on the sofa and gazed at the fire. Her voice slow and somber, "An infinite pain, you see, so traumatic it silences the victims."

"I'm not following," Bill sat at the edge of the sofa.

"Bill I think there's more to the killing of Wilbur Savage."

Dalton Ward's orb levitated by the staircase. He remembered the day Sarah brought Wilbur Savage to his home. He had pretended not to know him. He remembered their partnership, as he liked to recall, they definitely were not friends, just partners. Dalton's spirit squirmed near the lamp table jolting its side. The lamp wobbled on the tabletop. Bill and Margaret both glanced back at the table and then into each other's eyes.

"Do you think we have company?" Bill asked.

"Possible," Margaret relaxed against the back of the sofa.

Bill looked over at Margaret, her stare fixed on the fire. She seemed strong, unnerved by all the ghost events. He thought how lucky George was, to have her by his side all those years. He hoped to have the same with Liz. His eyes felt heavy as tiredness sunk in, each second a struggle to stay awake. Yet, his mind raced. He took one last look over to Clara and the chair before it faded.

*George, good fellow, you will have to stand watch, for now,* he thought.

George's spirit sat in the chair, back straight, stiffened into a perfect posture. His long legs stretched out in front of the chair nearly touching the coffee table. His hands rested mid thigh and his eyes fixed on Margaret.

Bill grinned, his eyes closed, he said, "You've never left her side, have you old fellow."

The three, Bill, Margaret and Clara slept as George watched over them.

Abigail's journey with Sara to the afterlife came to a halt when Dalton appeared before them.

"Brother-in-law what have you done?" Sarah asked with a timid voice.

Abigail did not move, and even if she could, she would not know where to go. She held Sarah's hand.

Dalton said, "You know not what you speak of girl!"

Abigail fell to her knees. She kept her eyes on Dalton. He was tall and thin and Abigail felt her chest sink when she looked into his eyes. He hid something, she was sure of it. The passageway to Liz and her daughter remained dark. Abigail listened to Liz's call, but it was quiet.

"Let us pass Dalton!" Sarah said.

The voices of many spoke from the darkness, *"Dalton let them pass,"* they said. Abigail forced herself to stand, and waited for Dalton's next move and watched as he faded into the background, that same expression on his face. Abigail knew it well.

# SEVENTEEN

Mary Elizabeth's arms hung between the jagged branches. Liz watched Wilbur's black blood seep through the roots of evil that held her captive. Its liquid traveled the child's body front and back, near her face and between her legs.

*This delicious angel*, he had said.

Liz grimaced and she held back the feeling to puke. She moved closer. She refused to take her eyes off Mary Elizabeth. She heard something, far away, someone calling her name.

A moment later she realized it was Abigail calling her name.

Alexandra's spirit moved around the room as Wilbur let out a wicked laugh. Liz searched the chamber for Abigail. Two people appeared in the distance, one of them a ghostly figure. The closer they came the larger they seemed.

"Abigail!"

Abigail ran toward Liz, the ghost of Sarah trailed. She reached the chamber they occupied and wrapped her arms around Liz.

"How did you get here?" Liz said.

"Sarah brought me," Abigail said, and then looked over Liz's shoulder and saw Mary Elizabeth. "Let her go!"

She peeled Liz's hands away and ran toward Mary Elizabeth.

"Abigail!" Liz yelled.

"Mommy," Mary Elizabeth said.

Abigail's body lifted up and flew past Liz colliding against the wall.

"No!" Liz said.

Alexandra and Sarah faced the wall that held Mary Elizabeth. Wilbur Savage was all around them, his evil spirit attached himself to Liz's family tree and from there he spread out in the underworld's endless space to create the hole he now used to hold them hostage.

*"Bring Dalton to me,"* he said.

*"Leave them be Wilbur!"* Dalton's voice came out of nowhere.

*"Dalton, old buddy, good to see you again,"* Wilbur's black blood rushed in between the roots of the tree as if he had a heart and his pulse rate increased.

*"Leave my husband alone!"* Alexandra squealed.

Wilbur laughed, *"Dalton, tell your wife how we met. Tell her about our friendship."*

Dalton's scream shook the area and sent Alexandra and Sarah flying. Liz and Abigail attempted to get up, but fell back on the floor.

*"We were never friends!"*

Wilbur hissed. His voice came from all areas of the space. Dalton knew he must destroy him or he would tell the secret they shared. He would lose his wife and Sarah if they knew. He held his secret for one hundred and twenty six years and managed to keep his wife by his side and raised two children after Eddie died. His role in the death of his son died with Wilbur. Now he searched desperately to find Wilbur, and shut him up for good.

Wilbur had always been resourceful. Dalton remembered back in 1885 Wilbur's ability to hide all things evidence, including what was left of the four small children that year. He remembered all right, his own confusion when Wilbur left his necklace by Eddies' beaten body. He remembered the epiphany that struck him during his own son's funeral. Wilbur wanted everyone to know their ugly secret. Had he known Wilbur's self-destructive ways he would have killed him when they first met, when Wilbur witnessed his own wrongful acts.

Dalton turned to see his wife staring at him, Sarah by her side. *"Dalton,"* Alexandra said, *"We must return the child to her mother."*

Dalton saw young Mary Elizabeth held against the backdrop of evil. An innocent child, whose destiny led to this moment. A curse executed by Wilbur Savage many years ago. He would make it up to her; protect her, as he protected Alexandra and Sarah all those years. His sins haunted him, but the only recourse was to keep Wilbur silent and then pose as the protector of his family, hide his ills for all time. That is how he has always done it. He looked at his wife again. Somewhere in her eyes, he saw uncertainty as Sarah leaned close to her.

*"Dalton?"* Alexandra said. She watched her husband and saw his reluctance to look her in the eye. Alexandra looked over Dalton's shoulder and saw Wilbur Savage as he use to look, young, on the handsome side, in human form. She didn't notice it back in 1885 but there was an evil there, somewhere in his eyes. She grabbed Sarah's hand.

*"Dalton,"* she said.

Wilbur ran his long decaying finger along side Mary Elizabeth's delicate skin, *"She certainly is beautiful,"* he said. *"Maybe I can wait for another time for the truth to be revealed."*

He looked back at Dalton and saw the look on his face.

*"You would be happy with that, wouldn't you Dalton? Allow the curse I put on you and your family to continue."* His sneer echoed throughout the chamber. *"To keep our secret."*

Dalton was silent; his eyes cold and fixed on Wilbur. Behind him his wife Alexandra remained silent, Sarah by her side with Liz and Abigail close.

"What secret?" Liz broke the silence.

The wave of Dalton's anger shook the ground. He turned toward Liz, eyes bulging and snapped, *"Shut up woman!"*

Liz took a couple of steps back. Her mouth fell open. She felt the need to hide but stood her ground. She thought of the curse Wilbur spoke of, and the secret Dalton keeps. Liz couldn't imagine what that secret would tell but if it's the only way to free Mary Elizabeth, then she knew the secret must be told. She felt her knees buckle underneath, but the coldness in her core moved her forward.

The curse of all Ward children made sense. Randy, raped as a child and grew up a serial killer whose path met with hers. Then there was Stan, a sick beast who claimed Mary Elizabeth as his own, her late husband Brad the pedophile that left many victims. She thought of Young Eddie Ward, whose fate Wilbur claimed. She looked at Wilbur; her lips squeezed tight, her fists clenched. She moved toward Dalton.

"I want to know the truth," Liz said. "What happened to young Eddie?"

"Liz," Abigail said in a whisper.

"It's ok Abigail," Liz said.

Dalton's spirit was silent as he hovered over Liz. His great granddaughter, strong willed and determined to get an answer. Times have changed. In his day, a woman would not be so bold. Images of his son flashed before him. A bright light appeared from the roots of the tree. Dalton looked into the gap between the hard rock and Liz's home office. The light grew brighter as it lowered into Wilbur's trap. Wilbur's blood swished about like singing birds; flowing through dead roots. He moaned as if pleasured when young Eddie appeared. His spirit protected by a white globe shield.

"My son," said Alexandra.

Young Eddie faced his father, but remained silent.

Abigail stepped closer, her eyes on Dalton. There it was on his face, in his eyes. The same look she saw in Brad's eyes when she was just a child.

"Liz," she said, holding on to her aunt's arm. "Something's wrong here."

"It's the secret, Abigail."

"Secret," Abigail said. Her face paled as she tried to focus, but memories of Brad hovering over her bedside kept her from speaking.

"Yes," Liz said as she looked over at Abigail. "Abigail, are you all right?"

Abigail allowed her hair to fall as she gazed downward shielding her face. She had her own secret and the thought of telling Liz terrified her. It has been years since her uncle molested her. Still, guilt and shame thrived inside her, crippling her ability to offer more than a one-word response.

"Yes," she said. She raised her head and saw her daughter pinned up against the wall, covered with Wilbur's evil blood and tree roots. She spoke, voice alarmed and rushed, "Dalton, tell the truth!"

*"You know not what you speak of child!"* Dalton snapped.

*"Father,"* young Eddie said. *"You must save Mary Elizabeth. She is your great granddaughter."*

The pleading look in Dalton's eyes weighing down on his son was too much for Abigail. "Tell the truth!" she said. "Tell Alexandra what you did to your son!"

*"Hush!"* Dalton said.

"God, how I know that pathetic look! You stand there silent but your eyes beg your son to keep quiet. Tell the truth! Break this curse you've bestowed on this family!"

Liz darted her eyes at Abigail, her throat, heavy and dry. She braced herself as she listened to Abigail's revelation. Of course, she spoke from experience, her niece, she took after her sister died, whom she loved like a daughter, talked about her husband. He violated her night after night and she never told. They never talked about it, whether guilt, shame or fear, their silence had been strong.

*"Enough!"* Alexandra's voice vibrated throughout the chamber.

Wilbur snickered as he watched the events unfold. Alexandra's spirit rushed toward the sound of his voice, her eyes bulged, her face transformed into something evil and dangerous. Wilbur's sly laugh, the only response he would give her, well executed, meant to enrage worked. Alexandra rose to the endless ceiling squealing like a banshee. Liz and Abigail covered their ears. Alexandra sped back down, striking Wilbur. The blast shook everything around them and loosened the grip of the tree roots holding Mary Elizabeth. Abigail shielded her eyes from the piercing light. Liz saw Mary Elizabeth fall to the ground. She rose to her feet and picked her up, cradling her in her arms. Sarah moved fast. She placed a protective shield to cover them and Abigail as her sister fought with Wilbur. When she turned and saw young Eddie, facing his father with his head hung and silent tears pouring down his cheeks the shield dissolved. She zeroed in on Dalton. Liz, Abigail and Mary Elizabeth huddled together vulnerable against attack.

*"Help my sister!"* Sarah said.

Dalton spun around and Sarah saw he was confused and vulnerable.

Though his spirit was weightless, he felt heavy.
"*Sarah,*" he said.
Liz and Abigail watched as Sarah turned her gaze away from Dalton. A man she held great respect for, whose grace was no more. Sarah could not look at him. Instead, she focused on Eddie. The pain she saw on his face left her without words.

Dalton's spirit faded as Sarah shunned him.

Alexandra's screams continued. Her cries brought Liz to her feet. She was no match for the likes of Wilbur, but adrenaline rushed through her body. A loud pounding in her ears masked Abigail's cries begging her to stay. Her head snapped back, chin up and arms extended out away from her body. Abigail gasped, but held her tongue.

Liz saw visions, one right after the other, of Eddie and through his eyes; she saw Dalton's sordid acts against him. The surrounding area, wooded, leaves whipped in the background as Eddie's frail body turned to face dirt, his father's breath heavy. She saw through Eddie's eyes a man in the distance walking toward them. She felt Dalton's evil sperm enter Eddie's body and heard his moans as he released his grip on him. His body jerked and moved away from Eddie when he saw the man, Wilbur Savage, close.

Abigail saw tears streaming Liz's face, but the tears were young Eddie's, as his father offered Wilbur Savage a turn. Her visions flashed forward in time and through Eddie's eyes, she saw Wilbur Savage walking across the front lawn with Aunt Sarah. Liz felt Eddie's heart stop.

# EIGHTEEN

The vision Liz saw last only a moment before she realized where she was again. She looked around the dark space and saw Abigail with Mary Elizabeth in her arms. Sarah faced young Eddie as he hung his head. Liz knew victory would be short lived. The curse upon them would end with the truth, and that truth had to come from Dalton.

"Dalton!"

She waited for him to appear.

"The truth Dalton!" she said and faced the darkness, her thoughts rapid. Wilbur Savage cursed her family because he wanted the truth revealed. She placed her hand on her stomach and closed her eyes. She looked back at Abigail. She had her own secret to deal with, but it would have to wait until they were safe.

It's crazy to think that way. She didn't know what was safe anymore. Normalcy as she knew it before didn't exist anymore. She knew that. Everything changed, including her new psychic abilities. She rested her eyes on Abigail for a moment. Her hair shielded her face as she caressed her daughter. A closer look revealed teardrops falling from her face, her jeans wet where the tears fell.

Liz said, "Dalton!"

*"Ask your husband!"* Wilbur said to Alexandra.

Liz whipped around to face Alexandra and Wilbur. Dalton didn't return when she called and Alexandra's screams scared the hell out of her. She rushed forward before she could even think of her own safety or of what she could do to save Alexandra. Alexandra's sphere spun around Wilbur Savage. His black blood gushed like a rapid river swirling in and out every crevice and cut through Alexandra. Her screams of pain caused Liz to scream, though scared out of her mind she prepared to fight. Liz's heart rate pounded her ears and the ringing sound seemed to mask everything as she thrust forward.

"Stop!" she yelled.

She entered into the swirling battle, her body stretched and twisted, her mouth opened wide. Her screams silenced, but Abigail saw her agony through the spinning wind of hell. Wilbur Savage threw Liz out of the battle. He laughed. Liz stood up and ran back to them. Abigail held her daughter close, shielding her view from the horrid scene.

Abigail needed to scream, but held back, she felt dizzy, she couldn't think. The noise stopped. She held her daughter with trembling arms and searched the area for Liz. All was dark aside, Sarah and young Eddie embraced in each other's arms.

"Liz?" Abigail's voice low and meek, she feared Liz was dead.

She saw a distant light. It appeared to move closer each passing moment. It grew brighter as it approached and when it was near, it turned black. It hovered over her and grew, covering what seemed like miles of thunderous clouds. His laugh lingered. Abigail shook her head back and forth. It can't be, Liz can't be gone. Wilbur loomed over them, hissing and snarling like a snake. His black blood was pulsing, his moans sickening. His pointed tongue slithered between his rotted lips. It's tip reaching Mary Elizabeth's cheek.

"No!" Abigail said.

*"Give me the child!"* Wilbur said.

Sarah and young Eddie joined Abigail and Mary Elizabeth merging with their flesh to protect them.

He neared with agitated breath. His desire overwhelmed his ability to move slowly. He would have Mary Elizabeth and then he would kill her and forever keep her for his sick pleasure. He laughed again as he thought about the curse. It would remain as long as the family kept their secrets and while they suffer, they will know he had Mary Elizabeth. One hundred and twenty six years he waited for Dalton to tell the truth. Now he had a different plan- wait another one hundred and twenty six years and let the Ward's suffer, the living and the dead would forever think of Wilbur Savage.

His groin of rotted flesh dripped and twitched as his tongue again reached Mary Elizabeth's cheek. She cringed. Abigail smacked it away and held her child close. She remembered when she was a child. Brad's thick tongue shoved deep into her mouth. The awful smacking sound of his mouth as he lay on her, raped her. Now this monster wanted to do the same to her child with his snake like tongue tasting her skin. She felt her rage coming on, could be a disaster she knew, but her face felt flush with every boiling second. She too could disappear like Liz if she loses it. The guilt and humiliation she felt as a child now replaced with deep seeded anger pushed her for the last time.

"There is no way you will take my child!" she said. She stood and stepped out of the protection Sarah and young Eddie provided. Her fists, balled tight hung by her sides. The strong and stern face of a woman who will take no more bullshit from Wilbur or the likes of him faced her threat. She couldn't cower, not now. Her gut told her she might die, and so be it. Enough was enough! She pounded her own chest with her fists, her words not yet formed.

She wanted to say, *Fuck you!* Instead, something compelled her to do what she never imagined she could.

"Liz!"

Tears soaked her red face. "He raped me Liz! Brad raped me!" she said.

As she turned and saw her daughter, her sweet innocent baby she said, "Mommy loves you."

Mary Elizabeth said, "Mommy!" She tried to run to her mother, but Sarah and young Eddie held her back.

Abigail faced Wilbur. His face larger than the room loomed over her; the acrid smell of death, his rotted filthy flesh didn't deter her.

Wilbur's hands raised up around her, *"You weak woman. What can you do to stop me!"*

Abigail raised her fists, "Come on you bastard!"

Wilbur drew closer, his mouth wide enough to devour her in one swallow. His horrid saliva dripped over her and slimed its way down the side of her face, reaching her chest. The thick liquid formed around her left breast. It squeezed her flesh, "Did you tell your auntie how much you loved your uncle when he touched you there."

"Get your filth off me!" Abigail said.

The darkness reminded her of her childhood bedroom, her memories of Brad sneaking into the room, his breath smelled of whiskey and cigarettes. His hands were cold and rough as he placed them over her barely developed breasts. She cringed and tightened all her muscles until he was done.

She looked at Wilbur. "Is that what you think, your victims liked your touch? You sick son of a bitch," she scorned. "They loved you so much you had to kill them to keep them from talking."

Wilbur flared his nostrils, *"Shut up woman!"* he snapped. His blood poured around her as if his heart rate increased, his saliva, a thick mucus laced with black blood rushed from his mouth and formed a puddle around her, twirling and spinning with her in the center.

Mary Elizabeth whimpered, "Mommy."

Wilbur raised both limbs stretching across the entire ceiling; his decayed fangs hovered just above her head. She heard Wilbur's blood and saliva moving around her. She lowered her body, her legs wide, ready for impact. Wilbur's eyes bulged from their deep sockets bearing down on her.

"No!" Sarah said.

Wilbur backed away from Abigail and moved toward Sarah. She froze, but held onto Mary Elizabeth and young Eddie, who hid his face against her body.

"Bad man," Mary Elizabeth said.

Wilbur directed his focus on Mary Elizabeth. Her youth captivated him, his desire overwhelmed him, and determination drove him mad. He will control the child.

Mary Elizabeth stared up at his face, her brown eyes innocent, absent of fear. She pointed her petite fingers and said, "Dalton."

Wilbur spun around and faced him.

Dalton's face didn't flinch a muscle. His eyes dead on Wilbur, his body tense. His desire, destroy Wilbur. He was flesh, in human form as he was in 1885.

Wilbur's sphere spun and rose to the ceiling. He dropped back down, and appeared as he was when alive.

Face to face, they both snarled.

*"I am a demon,"* Dalton said. *"I belong in hell."*

"No, no, no," Wilbur snapped. "You will not keep me from her!"

*"I violated my own son,"* Dalton muttered. He looked at his son peeking through small hands. *"Forgive me my son,"* he said.

Young Eddie clung to Sara.

*"I want my mother."* He said.

Dalton deserved rejection from his son. One hundred twenty six years of silence caused great pain for his family. Generations of children suffering abuse and shame, theirs and his, damaged lives. He was there, watching every wrongful act against his descendants. All of it had come to this moment when the living could bear no more pain, and joined his family in the afterlife. He shook his head and muttered words. A grimace replaced his angered face. He enjoyed his own pleasure of watching each assault on his descendants, what he could not do in death he vicariously accomplished. Each agonizing detail now repulsed him. It was time to end his madness.

*"You have the truth!"* he yelled. *"End this curse on my family!"* Dalton said.

Wilbur let out a growl. His sphere expanded, *"You have not told the entire truth! Tell them Dalton! Tell your family how much you've enjoyed their suffering!"*

*"Dalton?"* Alexandra appeared behind him, Liz by her side. She looked into his eyes and saw the guilt swell just before he looked away.

He wanted to lie, something he's done quite well over the centuries. Dark smog appeared around him as he glared at Wilbur. Again, Wilbur threatens to tell his secret, that's why he killed him, not out of revenge for his son. No, not that, truth was he didn't know what he would do to his own son if he threatened to tell. Wilbur's black blood rushed like a raging river from the walls.

Abigail looked up and saw Liz's home office above them.

"Liz, look!" She pointed to the gap and ran for Mary Elizabeth.

"Come on! Mary, climb sweetie. Go as fast as you can!"

Mary Elizabeth pulled herself up and looked back at Dalton and Wilbur.

"Don't look back!" Abigail said.

Liz gave Abigail a boost, "Go! Go!" she said. "There isn't much time!"

Liz grabbed onto the tree root to follow, but glanced back. Their eyes were dead on her, that of Alexandra, Sarah, and young Eddie.

"Liz move!" Abigail said.

Liz stared back at her ancestors and saw betrayal in their ghostly eyes. She grabbed another root and hoisted herself up; she grabbed another and turned her back on them. She had to believe they would be all right. Near the top she looked back down and saw them waving. After a long pained stare into Alexandra's eyes, she grabbed another root, her legs were weak, her sobs increased and then she looked up and saw a hand reaching into the dark pit, and then Bill's face.

# NINETEEN

The painted tree dimmed more and more over the last few months. There were no signs of Alexandra. Liz struggled over her decision to leave her in the afterlife. Her research revealed Alexandra's past, how she traveled to America, escaping certain death in Scotland. A young girl whose grandparents put her on the ship California after her parents died, a story untold or forgotten over generations. Liz wondered how many lives the curse affected before her time, and in her spare time, she searched for answers.

"Liz," Bill whispered behind her. "Come to bed. It's late dear." He placed his arms around her shoulders and kissed her head.

Liz took a long savoring breath, "Yes, it is late." She turned the lamp off and faced him, "Let's go to bed," she said.

They walked out of the room. At each lamp they paused, and turned off the lights, until they reach the top of the stairs and disappeared into their bedroom.

Abigail checked in on the girls as she did every night before she retired herself. Her footsteps quiet as she eased across the room, so silent she couldn't hear the creaks of her own feet pressing down on the aged flooring. She effortlessly left their bedroom through the closed door.

Margaret lay unconscious since pulling Liz and her family through the tree, her breath labored, sweat dampened her face, her expression a silent horror.

The ghastly scene replayed nightly in Liz's dreams beginning with her standing in her home office staring at the family tree and ending with her screams as she realizes they were all dead.

"No!" she said.

She sat up in the bed. Bill grabbed her arm, "It's just a dream," he said.

Liz cuddled next to him. Her heart beat fast as if she just ran for her life. She heard the deck furniture, drag across the concrete pad out back and slam up against the house. Her sweaty palms held the sheet tight, leaving it damp and wrinkled. She squeezed her eyes shut as he hovered over her. The smell of his cigarette and whiskey breath gagged her. He came every night, haunting her, and she knew why. His breath was close to her ear, she covered them with balled fists.

*Go away*, she said without speaking aloud.

The home office had been silent for months. No spark of life from the family tree, no new leads on their ancestors' either, nothing until this morning. Liz heard it from her bedroom. It came from downstairs. When she opened her eyes, she was alert, her vision clear and focused at the back of Bill's head. A half second later Liz whipped the covers to the side and stumbled her way toward the closed bedroom door.

"Damnit," she said. "I never close my door."

She turned the cold knob and yanked the door wide open. It slammed into the wall, but didn't recoil. Liz paused and looked back at the door. She smirked and continued down the stairs and skipped over the last three. The floor creaked as she sped toward the office. Her giggles were loud and giddy.

As she burst into her office, she shouted, "Alexandra!"

Daylight peeked through the curtains. The family tree stood pasted to the wall, dull and lifeless. Liz tried to grasp it all as she stood in the doorway. Her chest sunk, shoulders rounded. She leaned against the doorframe.

Under her breath, she said, "Alexandra." Her shrinking heart ached when she realized she was alone.

"Liz?"

Abigail stood behind her, coffee pot in hand.

"Liz, are you all right?" she asked.

No matter how hard she tried to keep the tears in, they escaped. Everyone, Abigail, Bill, Margret told her Alexandra was gone.

"Liz," she said in a soft voice. "Come have some coffee with me."

"I'll be right there Abigail," she sighed.

They told her she had to let go of the dead and move forward. She could accept that if she had not been to the other side. She was as alive as ever when she was in the afterlife. Scared as she was, she got a taste of eternity. Now she knows goodbyes are not forever. Unless, the dreadful thought choked her, they didn't want her anymore.

She wiped her tears and turned off the lamp. "Rest now," she whispered to her tree. Her exit was slow and soft; her hand grasped the doorframe as she paused there for a moment feeling something wrong. The ghost of Brad stood near the window of the small office in a dark corner watching her. His figure, sharp edges framed the outline of his large silhouette and he smelled of cigarettes and whiskey. He was easy to miss in the dark, but Liz knew that odor well. She turned her head and looked over her shoulder. She said in a confident tone, " I know you're here," and joined Abigail in the kitchen.

"We have a nine o'clock this morning." Abigail said.

Liz took a sip of coffee and leaned against the kitchen counter. "What's the background?" she asked.

"Mother of two teens, and an estranged husband, he comes and goes. Mother works in an antique shop. She spends most of her time there." Abigail sat her coffee mug on the counter. "Girls are home alone after school, until around ten.

"Is that when the activity happens?" Liz asked.

"No, it doesn't start until the mother gets home."

"Interesting, mother's past encounters?" Liz asked.

"She's avoiding the topic."

"Yes, she is," said Margaret.

"Good morning Margaret, coffee?" Abigail grabbed a cup without waiting for an answer.

"We may have to stay the night over there," Margaret said as she settled on the stool.

"Stay over night?" Bill said as he sat beside Margaret.

Abigail slid the coffee over to him, "Yes, Bill we have another client," she said.

"Business is good, then," Bill said. "How did they find us?"

"The newspaper ad," Abigail said and grinned at Bill.

Bill nodded his head, "That was quite an ad we came up with, Haunted?" he said with enthusiasm. "Let our team of Genealogists and Psychics help." He laughed, "Most people think we're crack pots. But what is that now, four, clients in three months? I'd say we're doing fine for a new business."

"It's a start," said Liz and then she kissed him on the cheek. "I'm going to see what I can find on the net." She filled her cup and went to her home office.

Abigail waited for her to leave and leaned toward Bill, "How'd she sleep?"

"Tossed all night," he said.

"Did she say anything?" Abigail asked.

"Not a word," he said.

"Margaret, do you have any idea who it is?" Bill asked.

"No, I think its Liz, who holds it secret," Margaret said.

Abigail reached for the cereal box from the cabinet and slid it over to Bill. "Did you notice she's not eating again?"

Bill poured the cereal in his bowl. Margaret grabbed the milk from the refrigerator. She placed it on the counter under a ray of sunlight that crept through the kitchen window. Abigail moved it away from the sun.

She grinned big, she said, "I don't know why we're avoiding the sun. We're not vampires."

"Excellent idea Abigail, I'll take the girls out while you two get ready," Bill said. He jumped up and washed his bowl at the sink. He looked out the window and saw a man over at the tree line. The stranger looked at him and turned to walk away.

"Hey you, wait a minute!" Bill yelled. He ran out the garage door and stopped at the yard's edge. The stranger had disappeared, leaving no sign behind that he was there. Bill came back through the garage and saw Abigail and Margaret standing at the window.

"That's the second time I saw him," he grumbled. "I can't catch him. He's fast, disappears before I can get to him."

Abigail and Margaret glance at one another and then looked back at Bill.

"What?" he asked.

"Bill," Abigail smirked. She said in a long drawn out voice, "Hello, seen any ghosts lately?"

Bill grinned, "Not since a second ago," he smirked back. "I know he's a ghost. You ladies aren't the only ghost seekers around here," he laughed. "Margaret, think he's here for Liz?"

"Yes, I do Bill."

Abigail gazed out the window over toward the tree line. "Well," she hesitated. "We know he's a male. That's a start."

"If I didn't know any better," Bill let out a chuckle. "I'd think he's trying to steal my girl."

"Relax, Bill," Abigail said. She turned her attention away from the window, laughing along with Bill she said, "Jealous over a dead man?"

"I guess it is pathetic."

Their humor continued as they walked out of the kitchen. Margaret eased toward the window and looked across the lawn. The grass was tall, wind breezed across its tips, a serene sway back and forth relaxed her until her eyes ventured to the tree line. The space between the trees, dark and menacing, topped only by the man ghost who stood in the foreground. The entity, daring as it was staring at her with an intense expression. Margaret closed her eyes. She tried hard to see through his eyes. Whoever this spirit was, his connection to this realm was through Liz.

"Our client's father burned to death in a house fire," Liz said.

Margaret stumbled back a couple of steps, her voice a high pitch, "Oh dear Liz, you startled me," she said.

Liz joined her at the window and looked out across the field, "It's beautiful isn't it?"

"Yes, Liz, it is a beautiful yard." Margaret said, "A house fire?"

"Oh, yes, she must have been eleven or twelve. A neighbor got her out according to the local newspaper."

"What about the mother?" Margaret asked.

"It was a father and daughter at the address when the housed burned to the ground. Her grandparents raised her after the incident. She married seventeen years ago. The two girls are her only children, nothing on her estranged husband."

Margaret glanced out the window. The ghost was gone. She said, "Any infamous ancestors?" She looked around the room before Liz could catch her.

"No, nothing notable," Liz said.

They both heard the little footsteps coming down the stairs, "Mary Elizabeth," Margaret said. She smiled big and held her arms open, "Good morning sweetie." Mary Elizabeth ran into her arms, "Big hug."

Abigail and Clara came strolling in, Bill right behind them. Margaret kept her eyes open, searching for anything ghostly in the house.

"Aunt Liz," Mary Elizabeth said. "Uncle Bill's going to take us shopping, but first we're going to have a picnic."

"That sounds like a wonderful plan sweetie." Liz smiled and gave her a quick hug and then smiled at Bill. He winked and smiled back, giving her the assurance she needed.

*How did I get so lucky?* She thought. *He's nothing like Brad.* She shivered at the thought of Brad. After what he did to her... and to Abigail, the bastard deserved to die.

"Liz?" Bill asked. "I asked if you would like to come with us on the picnic."

"Oh," Liz felt her face blush, "I would love to come along, but I'm needed here to prepare for our new client."

Abigail spoke up, "Liz, go ahead. We'll take care of things here."

Liz was about to take Abigail up on her offer when a loud pound on the front door surprised every one.

Bill opened the door, but there was no one there. He looked back at Liz with a perplexed look on his face, "We're hearing things or we have company."

"It may have to do with our new client," Abigail said.

Margaret stood back on the other end of the entryway, looking past everyone at the front door. He stood a good six feet tall, dark hair, vacant eyes. The smell of whiskey invaded the air, she yelled, "Shut the door!"

# TWENTY

Liz bolted to the door and slammed it shut before anyone else could move. She leaned her head against the cool wood and for a few seconds all she heard was her own breath, and her heartbeat thumping her eardrums. Her skin felt flushed, she thought her blood must have rushed to her vital organs, leaving her face pale. Only then did she feel the onset of nausea. *Oh god*, she thought, as she stood there numbed until her hearing seemed to recover with an astounding echo.

"Liz!"

She turned her head and saw them staring at her and she wondered what she must look like, holding onto the door. She felt the sweat trickle down the side of her face. Her chances of covering up the panic she felt was slim, but she didn't know what to say. Telling them the truth would damage their relationship, she felt blessed to have them, and desperately wanted to hide her dreadful secret.

"Liz, come on, come sit down," Bill's familiar hands held her shoulders and guided her to the sofa.

Liz moved slow as she tried to think of something to say. Her throat turned dry and when she sat, Margaret was across from her. By the look on Margaret's face, Liz knew she had an idea who was at the front door. The shock left her dazed and the second she cleared her throat a glass of water appeared in front of her. She followed the hand that held the glass and saw that it was Abigail.

"I have a headache. I should go lie down for a while." Liz said. She would do whatever it takes to keep the secret, including her current inability to look Abigail in the eye. She managed to get to her feet and wobbled until Bill caught her.

"I'll get you to bed," he said.

As Liz took those dreadful steps toward the stairs, she could feel Margaret's eyes on her. She tried to glance back at her but stopped short of seeing Mary Elizabeth, her little lips pressed tight, and Liz got the awful feeling that she also knew about her secret.

Liz darted her eyes at Abigail.

*Oh god why didn't I do something.*

But she feared she would lose her forever. She kept her focus on the floor until she reached her bed and even then, she closed her eyes tight. She wanted it all to go away. Bill closed the curtains and left the room, leaving her with her own thoughts.

He descended the stairs two at a time and met Margaret and Abigail in the living room. "Ok, who is he?"

At first, Margaret didn't say anything but when Abigail remained silent, she said, "He's Liz's husband, Brad."

"What. Brad. He's here?" Abigail balled her fist and pounded the air, "You bastard," she said.

"Great, my competition is dead," Bill announced.

"You don't have to worry about competition," said Abigail.

"So let's figure out what he wants and get rid of him," Bill said.

Margaret rose from her seat and held Mary Elizabeth's hand as she walked toward the kitchen, "He wants something from Liz," she said.

"Liz?" Bill followed her in the kitchen. "Abigail," he called. "Tell me about this Brad how was their marriage?" He turned toward her direction and thought it curious how she lingered in the other room. "Abigail," he said. She stood near the fireplace, hand on her chin, head tilted.

"In deep thought?" Bill asked.

Abigail dropped her hand and faced him, "Bill, there's something about Brad, but I think Aunt Liz should tell you."

"What is it?"

"Bill, please," Abigail folded her arms across her chest. "We never talk about it."

Bill grinned, "Well, see that's half the battle."

"Brad," she said and stopped short of telling Bill everything when she saw it. The outline of his body stood no more than five feet from her. In the outline, she could see through him as if he were made of amber brown glass. It could not be anyone else but Brad.

Bill saw her mouth fall wide open as she stared, "Abigail?" He said and turned his head. There, on the other side of the stairs, he saw something odd.

"That's new," he said as he examined the glass orb. It moved to the right and he could see the outline of a man, maybe six feet tall. "He's staring at me." Bill said.

Abigail said, "Yes, I think he is."

"Is it Brad?"

"Yes," she said.

Brad moved toward the stairs. He looked up to the second floor and then back at Bill. He faced forward and sure enough headed up the stairs.

"Liz!" Bill darted across the room. Abigail was right behind him. They each took two stairs at a time. Bill grabbed the door handle and burst through the bedroom door.

Abigail flew around him, and saw Liz asleep and unharmed. She stood at her bedside while Bill searched the room.

"No sign of him," he whispered, as Liz lay undisturbed. Bill watched as Abigail pulled the covers over Liz and thought how caring the two must be, to support each other the way they do. Together, they could survive anything and though Liz seemed troubled by something dark, she will get through it. She had too. He motioned Abigail out of the room. In the hall, he looked around for the glass figure and saw it was safe.

Bill said, "What was that?"

"I don't know, Bill," Abigail sighed. "But I know he'll return."

"Abigail, you must tell me about this Brad."

Abigail leaned against the hall wall. Her head tilted, looking toward the floor. She had been accustomed to silence about the assaults. She never talked to Liz about it, not even after she spilled

121

her guts in the afterlife. Abigail understood the pain they both held. When Liz didn't bring it up, she didn't want to push the issue.

"Bill, some things are better left unsaid."

Bill grabbed her arm, "What things? Because I think it's better to get it in the open."

"Bill, I can't tell you anything… not without Liz." She pushed herself away from the wall and rushed to the stairway.

"Abigail, please let me help," Bill called after her, but she kept moving down the stairs. "Damn it," he said under his breath.

He stood in the hall outside the bedroom door; on the other side, Liz lay awake and silent. A tear trickled down her cheek. Her face grimaced on top the pillow. How could she tell Abigail the truth? Vivid memories of her late husband sneaking out of their bedroom replayed each agonizing step.

*Please stop.*

She remembered how quiet, he was; he even avoided the creak on the flooring in front of Abigail's bedroom door. Liz lay there that night listening to his muffled moans as he lay with her niece. When he returned to her bed, he bounced hard on the mattress and yanked the covers from her, she could hardly breathe through the thick mucus that poured from her nose. She buried her face into her wet pillow until she heard his snore. Then snuck out of the room and made her way downstairs, where even at that distance she subdued her cries. At daylight, she peeked in on Abigail, and watched her gasped every few seconds. The child had cried herself to sleep.

Liz sat up in the bed, feet on the floor. Her chest felt tight, breathing restricted. She put the horror of that night far in the back of her mind, and carried on with her life as if it never happened. She never again touched her husband, even as he lay on his deathbed. She stood and waited for him to stop breathing.

Bill poked his head through the door and saw Liz sitting on the side of the bed, "Liz?" he said.

Liz jumped up, startled. Her hair hung shielding her face from him, *Calm down Liz*, she told herself.

"I'll be down in a minute Bill."

He closed the door, *Rape, incest and murder,* a curse. "If there is a curse on the family, it isn't over yet." He hurried downstairs.

Liz stood there, numb, not sure what to do. She raised her trembling hand and brushed the hair out of her face. The tears welled. She walked into the bathroom.

Brad watched her from the corner of the room. Summoned by Wilbur Savage to reveal Liz's secret. The same demon who, when he was alive possessed him, controlled him as he committed those hideous acts against children. Wilbur's presence was inside him and he enjoyed every act, every thrust. He thought he heard Wilbur moan a couple of times as he molested his victims, but he wasn't sure it was Wilbur because he too fulfilled his own sick desires. His only regret is that he died too soon. When he heard about Dalton Ward, that he pleased himself through the living as they raped and tortured their victims, he too wanted that experience, another chance. Wilbur Savage was his opportunity to have it all again. As he stood there in the dark, he could feel it, the desire, he'd soon have when he destroys the bond between Liz and her family.

Liz walked out of the bathroom and paused at the door. Her eyes swelled. She dropped the towel and left it lying on the floor.

"Brad, I know you're here." The room was dark and quiet. "I can smell you Brad." She sat on the side of the bed, her head hung. He said nothing, but sat beside her as he used to when they were first married, when they had serious things to discuss.

He leaned close to her, his hideous mouth at her ear.

*"Liz,"* he sneered.

Liz flinched. Her eyes closed, forehead wrinkled. How could this bastard show himself here. Her grip on the bed sheet tightened, she thought she'd puke right there.

"What do you want?"

Brad shifted to the other side of her, he said, *"I'm going to tell Abigail the truth."*

He moved in front of her and stared at her face.

"What are you talking about?" she scorned.

She felt something brush across her mouth. She squeezed the bed sheet, her feet placed firmly on the floor. She closed her mouth, and held her breath. He reeked of death. His cold tongue touched her lips. His face appeared, no more than an inch from her face. He grinned and then forced his tongue in her mouth. She gagged. Her hands flailed about as she tried pushing him away. Her arms went straight through him.

"No!"

She ran into the bathroom, plunged to the toilet and heaved until the vomit gushed from her mouth.

He followed and whispered in her ear, *"You knew."*

# TWENTY-ONE

"Please Alexandra, where are you?" Liz said. When awake she locked herself in her home office. She hadn't brushed her hair in days nor had she ate anything. Her notes lay everywhere trashing the room.

"Liz," Abigail said as she peeked through the door.

Liz held her head down staring at the floor. Her back turned away from the doorway and anyone who entered. Facing them now would only make it worse. She stared at the notes in front of her, "Yes," she said.

"Liz dinner is ready. Why don't you come join us."

"I can't just yet, too much work to be done."

"Ok," Abigail said. "I'll bring you a plate then." She closed the door and immediately joined Margaret and Bill in the kitchen. They both looked at her waiting to hear if she'd got anywhere with Liz.

"Nothing!" She threw her arms up in the air. "I'll fix her a plate. But I doubt she'll eat." She grabbed a plate and slammed it on the table. Margaret and Bill stepped back out of the way. Abigail yanked the silverware drawer open and grabbed a fork. Holding on to it as if she were going to stab someone with a downward thrust.

"Where the fuck is Brad! I know he has something to do with this!"

Margaret didn't say anything. But she sure had a lot of thoughts going on in her head. She watched Liz descend into self-pity. She agrees with Abigail; Brad has something to do with it, she suspected a dark secret. Her psychic abilities thrived when she, Abigail and Liz were helping clients, but when it came to Liz and her family, her powers proved useless.

Abigail slopped mash potatoes on the plate.

"You'd think that bastard would come after me, not her. He didn't have a problem coming after me the last time!"

She put the pan back on the stove and grabbed the fork.

"I'd be happy to take him on now."

She stabbed the chicken in the fry pan and brought it over to the counter above the plate. She jerked the fork to release the chicken, but the breast clung to its teeth. Bill thought he could see every facial muscle tightened as she beat the plate until the chicken fell from the fork.

Mary Elizabeth looked at Bill, "I think mommy's mad."

Bill smiled and leaned toward her, "I'll take care of her," he said.

Margaret reached for Mary Elizabeth's hand, "I could use some help setting the table." Mary Elizabeth smiled and followed her out of the room.

Bill took another plate from the cabinet and salvaged as much food as he could from the counter. He wiped it clean as Abigail stood by breathing hard.

"I'm going to go give this to Liz. When I come back, I want an explanation," he said.

"Ask Liz while you're in there," Abigail sniped.

He moved closer to her, his voice calm. "Liz isn't talking to anyone right now. You tell me what Brad did to the two of you."

He walked away with the plate in his hand. He wasn't going to take no for an answer. He entered the office, put the plate on the desk and kissed the top of Liz's forehead. He left her there without saying a word. He returned to the kitchen and saw Abigail biting her lips.

She said, "Brad didn't do anything to Liz."

Flashes of Brad walking into her room caused her eyes to blink.

"Liz has locked herself up in that office since his visit," Bill said.

"I meant he didn't do anything to Liz physically."

Abigail's voice squeaked. She glanced over at Bill and made eye contact. She looked down at the glass in her hand. "Bill," she took a breath, "Brad assaulted me when I was a kid."

"Assaulted?"

Abigail talked fast, "He raped me, at night when Liz was asleep."

The glass in her hand shook. Water splashed on the counter top. She took a sip.

"I wasn't the only one."

"You weren't the only one?" Bill raised his eyebrows, "What do you mean?"

Abigail sat her glass down and leaned both palms on the counter.

"When he died people started talking. Children," she gasped, "many children came forward and said Brad molested them."

Bill stood straight up; he tilted his head upward and closed his eyes for a moment. He's not usually stumped for words, but all he could think about is the pain Abigail and Liz must have suffered.

"Bill, Liz never talked about it."

Bill's forehead wrinkled, he made eye contact with Abigail.

"Not one word," she said.

There was a moment of silence before Margaret said, "Tables' set."

Bill didn't know what to think of Liz. Did it hurt her so bad that she couldn't speak about it? All this time? Even after she went to the other side?

"Bill."

"Bill," Margaret said again.

He swooped Mary Elizabeth up, "Well then, let's go eat," he said, then walked into the dining room.

Abigail took a deep breath. Her legs wobbled, yet she felt better. She smiled to herself, nodded her head standing there at the kitchen sink. Bill had become a close friend, the first person other than her dead relatives that she's confided in, "Whew," she said and joined the others in the dining room.

At the dining table, Margaret watched Bill play with his fork and Abigail stared off into space. Neither spoke.

"I've canceled appointments this week." Margaret wiped her mouth and laid the napkin on her lap. She looked over at Mary Elizabeth, who shrugged her shoulders and smiled. Margaret offered a smile in return and then announced, "Liz will be going to the other side."

Bill dropped his fork, "What?" He glanced at Abigail and over to Margaret, "When was this decided?"

Abigail placed both her hands on the table; she seemed ready to sprint out of the room. "She can't go alone," she said.

Bill pushed his plate away, "She's not going at all," he said.

"That too." Abigail said. She stood at the table, "I'll go check on her," she said.

Abigail rushed out of the room and passed through the kitchen. The living room was quiet. What was left of daylight barely peeked through the curtains. She paused for a second, her body shivered. There was a sound, something unusual. The room was empty yet she continued to search for the source. To her left the home office door was wide open.

"Liz," she said.

Each step she took was void of sound.

Something's wrong.

Just as she reached the office door the smell of whiskey and cigarettes burned her nostrils. It's Brad. She rushed into the office.

"Liz," she said.

Abigail froze as she fixed her sight on the family tree. The lone lamp shined bright facing its direction. She ran her hand through her hair as she leaned forward, there at the bottom of the tree, Brad's name was painted in red. "What the hell."

A closer look and she thought she saw the paint dripping. She leaned closer and reached her hand to touch it. The surface was wet. She pulled her hand back and rubbed the substance between her fingers. Something moved in front of her, she looked up and stumbled back. The branches of the tree swayed as if stormy weather intruded its once peaceful setting. Each painted name fluttered in its wake. Between the tree branches empty space spun, it reminded her of a funnel. The turbulence caught her off balance. She fell forward into the tree. A bright light flashed as she was sucked into the abyss.

Liz returned to her office and sat in the chair facing the tree. Her face puffy from crying, her stare distant and harrowing. The names a blur until she saw Brad's name. She could swear it smirked at her as she stood up to go get the paint remover. She'd wipe him out of existence, for good this time. When she turned around, she saw Margaret and Bill at the door, she immediately looked away and blocked their view of Brad's name.

"Where's Abigail?" Bill said.

Wary eyes peeked through the strands of hair covering Liz's face. "Abigail?" she said. "I haven't seen her."

"She came looking for you," Bill said. He looked back at the other end of the office and behind the door.

Liz watched him, but said nothing.

Bill said with a harsh tone, "Liz. Abigail. Where is she?"

She didn't know, of course. But her suspicions told her Brad had something to do with it. She faced the tree. Brad's name was still there beside her name.

Bill nudged her aside and saw Brad's name.

"Was that there before?" he asked.

"No," said Liz.

Bill felt heat flush through his body.

"I," Liz said, before Bill interrupted.

"Tell me what the hell happened," he snapped. Margaret stood at the door, silent. She suspected Abigail was in the afterlife. Bill turned to her, "Go find Abigail," he said.

"Bill, I think," she started to tell him.

His nostrils flared.

"I need a moment with Liz," he said.

Margaret knew there was no point in arguing, or reasoning with him. The struggle had to happen between them. It may be the only way Liz would open up and tell her story. She closed the door. Bill banged his fist on the desk.

He said, "Brad raped Abigail."

It was not a question.

Liz didn't know what to say, if it was a question she could simply say yes. She waited. She wasn't prepared for the next question.

"When did you know?" his voice demanding.

"Bill, please, you don't understand." She tried to walk past him. He snatched her arm and forced her back.

"When!"

Liz covered her mouth with her hand, but she couldn't hide the horror on her face. This was it. The moment she had to tell her shameful secret. Bill waited as Liz took in gulps of air, trying to pull herself together. She wanted to puke.

An eerie laugh behind her sent a chill through her, she looked back and when she turned to face Bill again Brad appeared behind him. His grin was revolting.

There's no way Bill would understand how she could lay in her bed and do nothing the night she heard Brad returning from Abigail's room. Her cheeks heated, she had to say something, but she couldn't tell him the truth, that she killed Brad.

Brad's evil eyes stared at her, taking pleasure in her pain. She could see it in his eyes. Liz turned and faced her family tree, placing her hands over the painted names.

It had not been said before, "I heard him," she said. "When he came back from her room."

She had suffered a lot of pain in past years after Brad but none as devastating as the blank look on Bill's face when she turned and faced him.

"What…" he fumbled for words.

He once looked at her with adoring eyes filled with life, hope, even love. Those same eyes staring at her, were now flat and cold.

# TWENTY-TWO

Silence is the worst part, at least that's what Liz thought until a few seconds ago. Staring back at Bill's glaring eyes absent the twinkle once there was a long painful moment. She couldn't take it anymore, tears welled her eyes. She spun her body around to face the family tree seeking answers from her ancestors, it's what she's relied on for years. Their names were blurred through her tears, but it didn't matter, because she knew everyone of them, her request silent, please help.

Bill couldn't wrap his thoughts around it all as he stood staring at Liz in disbelief. His lips parted as he went to say something, and it was strange to him, the whimper that escaped. He stepped back and went to walk away, he turned to Liz, he said, "How," his eyes shifted side to side, Liz was gone. The tree sparkled near the floor. His gaze followed the names, downward until he saw Brad's name and next to it Liz's, painted red.

"Margaret!"

Bill kept glancing back at the office door, and back at Liz's name. As soon as Margaret entered the room, he grabbed her arm and guided her to the tree.

"I only looked away for a second," he said.

Margaret said, "Liz?"

"She disappeared."

Margaret examined the tree, the wall's surface was solid. The portal, she decided, would only open when something compelled it to do so.

"What were you doing when she disappeared?"

"We were just standing here, I looked away and she was gone."

"Bill," Margaret used her scolding tone, "what were the two of you talking about?"

He covered his mouth, his words a mutter, "I can't believe it myself."

"Believe what?"

"Margaret," he swallowed saliva. "Liz knew."

"Knew what?" she said.

Bill raised his hand, "About Abigail," he said. "She witnessed the rape and did nothing to stop it," his voice trailed.

"Come, sit down Bill," Margaret guided him into the living room. She heard the uncertainty in his voice. He collapsed onto the sofa.

"Bill," she said. "Victims of rape and witnesses are often shamed into silence. Fear of being condemned and demoralized keeps them from reporting the rape, even talking about it."

Bill fidgeted on the sofa, "I," his voice trailed again into silence.

"Tell me what Liz said."

"She said she heard Brad when he returned from Abigail's room."

"What else?"

"Nothing, I turned away for a second. I asked her something, but she disappeared."

"What were you going to ask?"

"How Brad died."

Margaret stood up, her head lowered as she tried to grasp her suspicions. "Bill," her whispered words resonated with Bill.

"Bill, the curse on Liz's family started with a grave secret."

"Yes, I know, with Dalton killing Wilbur, what of it?"

"He killed Wilbur to keep him quiet about his own acts of incest."

"I don't follow," Bill said.

Margaret spun around and faced Bill, "The Ward's have been cursed for decades, many instances of rape and incest."

"Margaret, I don't follow?"

"The curse, Bill. They couldn't tell their secrets, they were shamed into silence."

"You're saying Liz was affected by this curse? That she couldn't do anything about Brad raping Abigail? She couldn't say anything?"

"No the rape is or was Abigail's secret."

Bill saw her eyes widen and her rosy cheeks turned a bright red, he said, "What?"

"Liz has her own secret."

"You think she was raped?"

"No Bill, I think she killed Brad."

Bill leaned forward and clasped his hands, nodded his head a couple times, and then sat back. "I'll be damned," he said. "That's why she kept quiet."

"Bill," Margaret said. She watched his sly grin return to his face, "Bill."

"Margaret." His grin wide, "That's the best news I've heard yet."

Margaret was quiet for a moment, as she looked dumbfounded at Bill. She nodded her head, "You do realize Liz could go to prison." She hoped to see Bill acknowledge the possibility. But he kept his grin and nodded his own head.

"Bill?"

"Margaret, dear, who's telling the police, us? Liz's dead relatives?"

Margaret hesitated at first, then said, "I see your point." Her cheeks reddened even more, she said, "I've never been part of a cover up. I wonder what George would think." Her thoughts carried her away and when she realized where she was again she turned her head toward Bill. His grin was gone. "What is it Bill?"

Bill jumped up from the sofa, he said, "We have to get to Liz. I turned my back on her."

"You've been here for Liz since you first met her, Bill."

"No, I mean in the office before she disappeared. I turned away." A terrible sense of loss hit him, he looked down at his hands, palms sweaty. His palms never sweat.

"Margaret," he choked. "I could lose Liz."

He stomped into the office, Margaret followed. Both stopped at the sight of Liz's name. Brad's name pulsated. Liz's name turned pink in color with a gray undertone.

"What does this mean Margaret?"

Margaret stepped closer to the tree. As she leaned forward, she said, "Her name, it's turning black."

"Yes," Bill said. "But what does that mean?"

"Bill, I suspect when it does Liz will be trapped on the other side."

"How long do we have to reach her?"

Margaret straightened up and walked out of the office. Bill stood there. He looked at the tree and then the doorway.

Margaret poked her head back in, "We have to hurry, before it's too late."

She disappeared again.

Bill said, "What do you mean before it's too late?" He darted through the doorway. "Margaret, do you mean she'd be gone forever?"

"Yes, if her name turns the color of her ancestors she will remain on the other side."

"You mean she'll die?"

Margaret's silent stare struck him hard. He couldn't accept losing Liz. He felt a nagging pain in the back of his throat as he replayed the moment he turned his back on her.

"Damn it Liz," he sighed. "I love you."

"Bill," Margaret yelled from the dining room. "We have to hurry!"

***

Liz fell into Brad's personal chamber. The place he'll spend eternity, tormented by his unexpected and early death. The smirk on her face seemed unfitting considering she now stood where he'd be more powerful. The chamber, not at all like the one Wilbur possessed, except for the feeling of impending danger, had one item displayed. A small flask she recognized as soon as her eyes adjusted to the darkness. Though strange considering she stored the damn thing in her attic when she first moved into the house. Nonetheless, there it was, laid upon what looked like a photograph.

Caution Liz, he's here somewhere, she reminded herself as she stepped forward to get a look at the photo. A few steps closer and she stopped moving and listened to the chimes. It wasn't long before she realized it was her own, the one she left behind when she moved out of her old place. The house she and Brad shared for nearly thirty years. She looked down at the floor and saw blue Berber loops, her old carpet.

"You turned your death chamber into our old house."

*"My house Liz."*

Liz stumbled back and searched for him, seeing nothing but a façade of her old home. She crept closer to the flask and saw it wobble from side to side. The photo underneath outlined a person, moving closer she saw the person was herself. She glanced around then refocused on the flask. Inside the glass container was the poison she used to kill Brad. A secret she's never told anyone. Brad deserved to die and she'd be damned if she'd spend one day in prison for killing him.

She remembered the night she slipped the cyanide into his whiskey glass. He had just arrived home, from where she had no idea. She stood in the kitchen and listened to his footsteps when he went upstairs to shower. Above her, she heard the creak of the floor at Abigail's room, the quiet thump of his footsteps as he crept to her bedside. As she listened to his footsteps and waited for the pipes to fill with his shower water, all she could see was the poison in her hand.

*"Liz."* Brad said.

Liz's arms flailed. If Brad had any breath at all she would have felt it in her ear.

*"Drink it,"* he snickered.

"Go to hell," Liz snarled.

The flask shook. Liz watched it spin. She'd kill Brad again. If she could.

"Why bring me here Brad! Why not just tell everyone I killed you!"

He never did anything that made sense to her.

No regrets she told herself. Except, as she stared at the flask she thought of Bill. She had seen herself growing old with Brad when she was young, maybe she settled, but that doesn't matter anymore. When he forced his filth on Abigail something changed, perhaps her soul. At the time she wanted him dead, and somehow it seemed right. Now, as she stood there, still staring at the glass container halfway filled with the same poison she used to kill Brad, she thought it was cruel to find Bill only to lose him.

She squeezed her eyes shut and when she opened them the flask was gone. Nothing but darkness surrounded her, she couldn't see her own hands stretched out in defense or reaching for a wall or anything to hold on to, all she heard was her own rasping breaths. She kept reaching and reaching, she thought she saw something. Nothing was there. Nothing to grab on to and so she covered her face. Every muscle tensed as she waited. She heard a cry. The whimpers were weak, but Liz was sure she heard them. Again the cry came from somewhere in front of her, she strained her eyes to see a silhouette of a person. As she moved closer another whimper chilled her blood as it rushed through her body to her core.

"Abigail!"

Abigail sat on the cold floor, curled, face covered with her pink and white childhood blanket.

"Abigail!"

Brad, transparent as glass appeared out of the darkness and hovered over Abigail. His laugh sinister.

*"Liz,"* his voice seemed to come from all parts of the chamber. *"Tell Abigail about the night you heard me in her room."*

Liz offered a meek, "No."

Brad lowered to Abigail, his smirk never left his lips as he whispered something in her ear. Liz watched helplessly as Abigail reached her hands forward and crawled. The pain she saw on her face, the way her mouth hung open as if she wanted to cry, the way she stood and faced her, arms clutching her stomach. Her words.

"Liz, you tell me he's lying."

## TWENTY-THREE

"Abigail, please let me explain." She tried to steady her breaths. *I can't lose her.*

Abigail raised her hand to her forehead. "Oh my god," she said.

Liz stepped closer, "I have to tell you what happened to me that night."

She realized her stupid word choice when she saw Abigail's hands lift up above her head and the nod of disbelief.

"Wait Abigail," she said.

Abigail paced, made a circle and cupped her hand over her mouth. She glanced back at Liz, sprinted a distance from her, stopped and bent over to puke.

Liz's long held grimace hurt her jaw.

"Abigail, I swear to you it was the last night he touched you. I didn't know until then."

"And you did nothing! How could you do that to me!"

Her gruff voice echoed throughout the afterlife and to Alexandra, who remained in solitude after her husbands' secret was revealed. Abigail's cries triggered her memory, back to 1885, to the moment when Alexandra looked at her own sister, Sarah, and said, *"You brought that man to my house!"* Back to that moment when she and her sister separated for life.

Had she and Sarah stayed together, she may have learned of her husband's incestuous acts sooner. Certainly not after she'd spent nearly a hundred and thirty years believing in him.

The space surrounding Alexandra was empty. Was this her destiny? To spend eternity alone. She blinked her eyes as she listened to Abigail's rage, followed by Liz's pleas. Her thoughts were both solemn and paralyzing. She raised her head, with her eyes closed, her hands lifted upward as she reached for something more, something to save her soul from the depths of despair. She opened her eyes and her spirit rose above the weighted floor that held her captive.

*"My son!"* she said.

All the others stirred, awakened from their nothingness as the news spread among them.

*"It's Alexandra,"* they whispered.

Alexandra's fiery spirit was back! Her shrills reached across dimensions as she sped to her son, piercing blue eyes trailed by her white gown until she came to a screeching halt facing him.

*"Momma,"* he said as he gazed at her with affection. His hand touched her face, allowing her into his memories. His pain as his father violated him, the first time he laid eyes on Wilbur Savage, and when his father offered him over to him. She felt his horror when Wilbur raped him and left him alone to take his last breaths. A tear fell from Alexandra's eye and made its way to the ground as her son revealed more. After death he endured abuses by Wilbur until his father died and joined them in the afterlife only to take over where Wilbur stopped. It wasn't until she joined him in death that her first-born was freed from the torture.

Young Eddie repeated, *"Momma ... I love you."*

A single tear fell from Alexandra's eye and burst on the ground into hundreds of droplets, then spread out and rose up floating around her. In each drop were little scenes that led to this moment. Her roar shook the afterlife. The teardrops froze in mid air and there in one reflective drop she saw Liz. Her moment had arrived. Just as she and Sarah had separated Liz to would be separated from Abigail. The pain within Liz was now Alexandra's, and she said, *"My granddaughter."*

The tears burst again into millions of droplets and spread out, in each a scene replaying moments of forewarning, like when her husband never looked her way when he left with her son for the last time.

Alexandra peered into each scene. Each droplet returned to her eyes with bits of knowledge entering her soul. Her eyes were wide as she received the sinful signs of the wrongdoers. Those who committed sexual abuse against her kin. Soon the sparkles of knowledge entering her turned into a bright light and when complete Alexandra stood tall. Her eyes pierced through all who dared to question her new power, for she knew everything about them. Alexandra, the mother, warrior of all descendants, turned to face Liz. Her mother's face appeared to her and through her eyes the sins of her own father, retold with disclosure of her mother's murderous act against him.

*"Mother, I love you,"* Alexandra said.

*"Go, my daughter."*

Alexandra's spirit rose above all others. From her, one teardrop of love fell upon them, with the curse lifted their orbs shined bright as they wished her farewell. She traveled at a speed only greatness could achieve and stopped near Liz.

*"Granddaughter."*

Liz was on her knees, hair covering her face. Cries echoed throughout the chamber. Her head moved back and forth as tears fell from her face.

*"Granddaughter."*

Liz stood up. Her shoulders slumped. Up above them through the portal to Liz's world, Alexandra heard Bill and Margaret calling Liz's name. A short distance away Abigail seemed lost in a trance.

Alexandra noticed Liz's fingernails were growing dark, a sign of death. She didn't have much time before she'd forever remain in the afterlife, as she is now, alone and shamed. Alexandra sped to Abigail and hovered above her, she released one tear drop. The lens into the past showed Liz standing over Brad as he slept. She poured the colorless poison into his whiskey glass and lay beside him, her eyes wide open. Abigail awakened from her spell. Memories of Liz holding her close when Brad died, her words, "I'm sorry."

*Liz killed Brad.*

Abigail gasped and reached out to Liz as Alexandra hovered above her, "Aunt Liz," she said. "You killed Brad. For me."

*"Go child!"*

Abigail ran, heading for Liz at a speed Alexandra thought only she could accomplish. Liz moved further and further away. Her nails grew long and wicked, her hair wild, face covered, shoulders- a skeleton of the woman she use to be, Abigail screamed, "Liz!"

Alexandra hovered above them.

The closer Abigail got, the further she was, "This fucking world sucks!" she said.

She kept screaming Liz's name as she ran toward her, to the one person who avenged Brad.

*I have to save her.*

Abigail's heart raced and ached. She collided into an invisible wall. Her body flew up into the air and suspended as Brad's face appeared in front of her. His grip was tight. The smirk and foreboding glare of madness ripped at her. Beyond him Liz stood unveiled. Sorrow replaced her once loving eyes. Tears of blood poured down her pale, wrinkled, dead skin.

No!

Brad released Abigail's body into an endless abyss. Arms thrashed as she fell, her roar heard throughout the afterlife. She snagged the root of a tree and hung there to catch her breath. The long dark tunnel she fell through reeked rotted human remains. A guttural roar escaped as she grabbed another tree root. Above her, a glow emanated from Alexandra and beneath her total blackness.

Alexandra spread her arms wide. Her angry blue eyes focused on Brad. Wilbur appeared beside him, his laugh superior.

*"Come!"* Alexandra commanded. *"Come see them as they are!"*

They came from all sides and surrounded them. Their soulful eyes fixed on Brad and Wilbur, thousands of ancestors including Sarah and young Eddie. Alexandra floated above them. Her face enlarged spanning the edge of the crowd ready to learn the truth.

Abigail climbed up the soiled roots. The sound of Bill and Margaret's chants as they performed the séance empowered her to move faster. From a distance she appeared alien, her four limbs worked in unison as she ascended the top of the endless pit.

She had little time to save Liz.

Alexandra gazed down at Abigail. The expression of a mother's love on her face met Abigail's eyes. A tear formed and stretched across the congregated souls and levitated above them and they raised their heads, three thousand spirits waited for the truth to fall from their mother, Alexandra.

Abigail lowered herself, eyes on Liz; hands touched the ground, as she prepared to sprint. Ancestors surrounded her, the tear of Alexandra sparkled and broke into millions of tiny teardrops and descended on her family.

Over to her right, her own mother smiled and mouthed, I love you. As the teardrops fell on the spirits their hearts opened to receive the truth about their abusers, their devious plans and acts that hid their hideous crimes against children.

Abigail's timing was impeccable. Foot planted well on the rotted soil, she sprinted. Alexandra watched from above and proudly thought, *she has my speed.*

A tunnel formed by her ancestors spun around her and blocked Brad's attempt to stop her. At the end of the tunnel stood Liz. Her hair mangled white, tears of blood trickled down her black gown, filthy claws gripped the flask of poison.

Abigail wanted to scream her name but there was no time. She kept running. The tunnel's end nearing, her pace quickened. The impact sent both flying above their ancestors into the dead space. Abigail grabbed the flask from Liz's hand.

Liz's only words as she looked into Abigail's eyes, "I killed Brad," could have been her last. Abigail held her close, and their eyes locked as Alexandra watched.

Abigail held the flask out, smiled at Liz, and let go. Alexandra flew by snatching the flask in mid air. She paused and grinned. Her face turned pale, eyes wicked, her focus on Brad. She sped to him and grabbed his head. She forced his mouth open and poured the poison in and watched him shatter.

A female spirit, centered among three thousand relatives, lifted her face to receive a single teardrop that splashed on her forehead and entered her eyes. A vision from the past, her husband took her daughter to the playhouse, many times. Her daughter turned her head and glanced back, eyes sad. The female spirit turned her head and glared at her husband. His horrid secret traveled throughout the crowd. No words came from her. No cries left her soul. Her attack was vicious.

There were many attacks as dark secrets came to light. Alexandra floated above Liz and Abigail, her peaceful and loving eyes rested on them. They followed her gaze to the portal, back up the treacherous roots of Liz's hand-painted family tree. Liz and Abigail reached for Alexandra's hands and grasped tight and she led them toward the light, to the lone lamp in Liz's home office. Below the family battled. Spirits lifted upward and headed for the light, the place where their souls would rest for eternity.

*"My daughters,"* Alexandra said. She smiled and raised them up to a root close to the portal's rim where they could hear Bill and Margaret chanting. They grabbed the thick root and climbed to their world. Alexandra's screech shook the walls. Liz and Abigail stopped their climb, up over them Alexandra's arms stretched out, claws replaced her gentle hands, her hair wild, eyes bewildered. Below, Wilbur Savage stood amongst the remaining family members. He reached his long decaying arm out, his hand hovered over the head of a small spirit, a child. Lust crossed his evil eyes.

# TWENTY-FOUR

The clawed hand gripped the child's head, her eyes rolled back, whites exposed. Her mouth open, a stretched silent scream.

"Liz, it's Wilbur Savage!" Abigail held the root tight. "Liz!" she said, as she reached for her hand. "Come on, we're almost there!"

Abigail reached for the next root, her hand slid down its slimy surface. A thick sap formed a bubble and descended into the endless pit. Above she could see Bill and Margaret, "Liz!"

Liz stared downward, her ancestors battled to claim their peaceful afterlife. Alexandra squealed a horrid sound, face grayed, eyes darkened. If Liz didn't know her, she'd be terrified. Her great grandmother prepared for what could be her final battle.

Liz gazed at her own hand clasped in Abigail's, her eyes ascended the slender arms upward until she stared into Abigail's eyes.

"I can't leave."

"Liz," Abigail pled but she saw in Liz's eyes, she wasn't coming with her, and when Liz let go of her hand her stomach shuddered. She may never see her again.

"Go Abigail," Liz said.

Abigail watched Liz as she let go of the root and fell to a ledge on the other side of the pit.

Bill wrapped his warm hand around Abigail's wrist.

"I have you. Climb up," his voice anxious and angry. He lifted Abigail from the sodden root.

"Liz?" Bill asked.

"She let go of my hand."

Abigail looked around at the familiar space, her hand pressed flat against her heart. A short relief until she remembered Liz. She faced the family tree and rushed to the portal. The cool surface beneath her palms was now solid.

"Liz!"

Abigail slapped the wall several times and turned to see Margaret and Bill. Each with long faces staring at her with disbelief in their eyes.

"What happened Abigail? Why isn't Liz with you?" Bill's voice shaken.

Abigail studied the circles under his eyes as he leaned over her. He asked again about Liz, rushing her to answer.

"Bill, I don't know how to explain it to you, it's a real world there. Alexandra, she's real."

"I understand that Abigail. But why isn't she here?"

"Slow down Bill," she raised her hand from her hip and ran her fingers through the strands of layered hair, and held tight as she pressed her balled fist against her head. "She couldn't leave things unfinished."

"What things?"

"Damn Bill, let me think."

Bill raised his hands, palms wide open, "I'm sorry."

"The portal is closed for now," announced Margaret. Her open arms guided them into the kitchen.

Abigail followed as she stared at her own feet. Tea would calm her stomach but as she kept replaying what happened in her mind. The urge to go back and help Liz tore at her heart. Margaret helped her to her seat at the kitchen counter.

Bill reached for the teapot and filled it with water from the spout.

"I should have stayed."

Abigail's voice, quiet and desperate, worried Bill. He placed his hands on her shoulders he said, "Dear girl I hope you mean you should have stayed here. You can't be thinking you should stay where Liz is now." Her eyes welled with tears as he stared into them.

"It's not your fault," he said.

"Of course it isn't," Margaret interrupted. "I suspect this meeting of the two worlds, ours and the afterlife, was bound to happen. Your family endured this curse for decades. It's time to end the abuse. Now tell us Abigail, what happened there?"

"I was confused at first." she raised her head and nodded, "Even now."

Abigail shifted in her seat and sipped at her tea.

"It's foggy. I wasn't well at first, I don't know, lost. Liz came. She told me about Brad."

"What about Brad?" The detest in Bill's voice apparent.

Abigail rubbed her hands on her pant, her eyes fixed on the counter top. "After Brad," she paused.

"After that bastard assaulted you," Bill said.

"Yes, after that Liz poisoned him."

"Poisoned him?" Margaret's chin raised, her eyes narrowed.

"It was months after he assaulted me when he died. Liz had been poisoning him the entire time. I remember now how sick he was, how he stayed in bed. Evil bastard." She grinned at Bill.

Bill grinned and said, "That's more like it."

"His cause of death?" Margaret asked.

"Well, he wasn't poisoned, at least not to authorities. No one knew," Abigail said, "Not even me. She killed Brad for me."

Bill's grin grew wider.

"She told you that?" Margaret's eyes squinted.

"Yes. Well, actually, Alexandra did. When she did the trance I was in lifted. Alexandra came and cried over everyone. Her tears told a lot of secrets. A war broke out down there. Liz and I were climbing the roots, on our way to the portal."

"Wait," Bill said, "Alexandra's tears told a lot of secrets?"

"It's different there Bill, anything is possible."

Abigail found it difficult to explain, but it all made sense there. Bill sighed, "So why didn't Liz come with you?"

"I suspect she couldn't leave Alexandra to fight alone," Margaret's tone firm.

"What do we do?" Bill wanted to hear her say they'd go get her and bring her home.

"We wait." Margaret said.

"Wait," Bill moaned. His chest ached when all he could do was wait.

"I wonder what she's doing right now," Abigail worried.

"I assume she's fighting a demon," said Margaret.

"Wilbur Savage to be exact," Bill said.

Far yonder than most people traveled while living, over in the afterlife, Liz headed toward Wilbur Savage. Roots and thick black sap weighed her legs down. The sap stretched and snapped as she work her way through, careful not to fall. Wilbur devoured the small child's head. Liz's ancestors scattered around her, some managed to escape the once pedophile now demon in the afterlife.

"You don't deserve to be here," Liz said. "You belong in hell!"

In an instant Wilbur hovered over her, his cold eyes glared. Liz faced the demon, her stare unyielding. Her stance wide, fists by her side, her nails cut into her palms as she prepared for attack. Wilbur's square jaw moved side-to-side, sharp uneven teeth protruded his blackened mouth. Liz didn't flinch. Evil roots sprung from below and wrapped around her legs, still she stood, unafraid.

Wilbur hissed.

Liz heard it from all directions.

His filthy nails crept up her back, black saliva spilled from his mouth, and pooled around her. The acrid odor filled Liz's nostrils and burned her throat. Yet, she stood unwavering. Her goal was to distract him while Alexandra prepared for the kill.

Wilbur opened his mouth wide, ready to destroy.

"You have to be the dumbest fucking demon in hell," Liz said.

Wilbur closed his mouth and he drew his head back. Under him Liz stood trapped by the roots of the tree. Her tree. Above them an ominous haze of ash spun. Both aware of its arrival, but when Wilbur lowered his head, he saw Liz's smirk.

Liz raised her hands and pointed to the ash above, she said, "This is my tree!"

The roots snapped off her legs and freed her. Wilbur's snake like tail rose from behind him and struck Liz. She flew into the darkness where she lay unconscious.

Alexandra's face appeared out of the ash, her mouth wide. Her power, strengthened by the telling of all the secrets her family held onto, the sins, the suffering endured for decades, all of it entered her soul. Rage replaced vulnerability. Her roar shook the afterlife.

Her love for Liz is eternal, for it was she who paved the way, who killed her husband for his unforgiving sin. It was she who opened the portal to the truth. Her eyes softened when she gazed at Liz lying limp. Alexandra summoned the roots of their tree.

*"Wrap around her and take her back to the world of the living."* And so the spirits rose from the immoral soil. Their bright green roots draped Liz's unconscious body and hoisted her upward, each tip of ancestors touched her to say goodbye.

Alexandra turned to Wilbur Savage. He glared at her, but she wasn't fazed. His wicked black limbs grew to thousands and circled around her, his blood pulsed out of them and dripped like acid upon her. Each drop sizzled when it touched her spirit, and dissolved into tiny crystals of light that floated around until they settled on the ground, and from them blue violets sprung. Alexandra widened her mouth over Wilbur's head. Her jaw snapped shut with his head inside her mouth. He tried to free himself, but his limbs disappeared one after the other until he was gone.

Alexandra stood with her relatives, at peace. Her son on her right, her sister on the other side. She watched as the spirits danced among the blue violets, once victims, turned angels. She knelt by her son, *"Son,"* she said. *"I have to return to the living."*

Little Eddie hung his head, *"Mother, please, stay with me."*

*"I am always with you my son. When it is safe I will call for you to play in the meadow with Mary Elizabeth."*

Young Eddie smiled and took his Aunt Sarah's hand. Alexandra lifted herself up the roots through the portal to Liz's home office, where she stood guard by the painted family tree looking out onto the long narrow yard.

She heard Mary Elizabeth in the other room say, "But when will Aunt Liz be awake?"

Bill said, "Soon, now lets make her a wonderful gift shall we?"

Alexandra dared not wake Liz. She needed her rest.

Margaret and Abigail pulled out of the driveway in Liz's Honda. Their next client, a woman with a five year old child troubled by what her mother claimed to be an evil ghost. Alexandra sensed the child's father had violated her. She also sensed the arrival of another demon.

# TWENTY-FIVE

Liz felt the bed covers, hugging her body, the bed under her. She opened her eyes. The hall light shone into her bedroom.

"Home," she murmured.

She drifted back to sleep, dreamless. Her eyes opened again, same scene. Exhausted, she fell asleep again, this time her mind aware of the hall light. She opened her eyes. Darkness overwhelmed her as she lay there waiting. She blinked her eyes.

*Please let the light be on.*

It's dark.

Her body pinned to the bed, eyes wide. The pressure on her chest left her breathless, mindless of anything else. She closed her eyes and opened them again. The hall light was on and she could breath. Startled, she sat straight up, hands placed on the bed firm. Sunlight brightened the room.

*How long had it been daytime.*

Sweat dripped between her breasts and she tried to steady her breath. She tossed the covers to the side and listened.

Nothing.

Her feet dragged across the carpet. The cold bathroom floor felt good, at least it was a place to gather her thoughts.

*Had it all been a dream... everything.*

She looked in the mirror at herself, she appeared sick. After a moment she realized the weeping sound was her own. Her grip on the sink, threatened to crush it as she looked around for Bill's aftershave and razor. She rocked back and forth. This can't be. She told herself.

*I can't be alone.*

It dawned on her, she hadn't checked the rest of the house. Her legs wobbled as she darted out of the bathroom. She saw her bedroom door closed.

"Damn it, I never close my door."

Please, please let them be there. The upper level hall was quiet, the bedroom doors closed. Continuing forward over the ledge of the first stair she saw her living room empty.

*One step at a time Liz.*

A few more steps and she could see her fireplace. The wood sat on its grate unlit, the wrought iron tool set unused. Stepping down the stairs, her kitchen would soon be in view, her body tingled and her stomach felt empty. She held the banister tightly, leaving a trail of sweat as she slid her hand downward. The kitchen came into view as she descended the stairs.

Nothing cooking. She thought.

The sound of the garage door scared her, she held the banister with two sweaty hands standing at its base, her mouth fell open, there in her kitchen was Abigail and Margret.

"Bill. You here?" Abigail said.

"Yes, we're here."

He appeared out of the dinning room with Clara on his hip. Mary Elizabeth flew past him.

"Mommy!"

"We were making Liz a gift," Bill said with his usual self-confident grin.

Abigail looked down at Mary Elizabeth, "You were, how thoughtful," she said.

Teary-eyed Liz gazed at each one, "They're here," she sighed.

She and Margaret made eye contact. Margaret smiled.

"She's not awake yet?" Abigail asked.

Bill nodded his head over toward the stairs. He went to speak, but took a quick look back at the stairs and caught his breath. He handed Clara to Abigail without taking his eyes off Liz. His pace was slow at first, and then he sped up thinking she'd disappear again.

Liz's knees buckled on her as she moved forward. She could hardly believe her eyes. She reached out to him and grabbed his shirt and welcome his arms wrapped around her.

"I wasn't sure," she said.

"Sure of what Liz?"

"That this wasn't all a dream."

"It's not a dream Liz. We're all here."

He took her hand and led her into the kitchen. Margaret's chin was tilted high, her nod of approval put Liz at ease.

Abigail smiled big, and embraced her, crying.

"I thought I'd never see you again," Liz said. "I was scared, so scared. I'm sorry I didn't say something to you about Brad. I didn't know how."

They held each other tight for a long moment. Abigail pulled back, she said, "Hey Aunt Liz," she said, "we make a good team." She leaned her head on Liz's shoulder.

"Welcome home Aunt Liz."

Liz looked down at Mary Elizabeth, "Thank you, I'm happy to be home. Now what's the gift I heard you made for me."

Mary Elizabeth held her hand and pulled her into the dinning room.

"This way Aunt Liz," she said.

Bill whispered, "Well, what do you think. Is she ok?"

I think she's alright Bill." Abigail's voice hopeful.

"I can tell you there aren't any threatening spirits." Margaret hadn't felt anything negative since Liz came through the family tree and landed beside the lamp.

Bill had to ask, "Brad?"

Abigail laughed and whispered, "No Bill you won't be seeing Brad again."

Liz entered the kitchen with a poster size hand-painted family tree. On it was Liz, Bill, Abigail, Margaret, Clara and Mary Elizabeth. She taped it to the refrigerator. She said, "We also won't be seeing Wilbur, Dalton, Stan, or Randy."

Margaret interrupted, "Yes, they are gone, but we will find others."

"Liz," Abigail said, "We have people calling from all over the state. They want our services."

Liz looked over to Bill, his eyebrows raised, his grin wide.

"Are you in with us?" Liz said.

"I wouldn't miss this for the world."

He took her hand and walked her to the front door. "Not even for your hot apple pie, or those glorious blue violets."

Liz peeked at the blue violets and saw them sparkle in the sunlight. Her ancestors were close. They're always close.

"Alexandra?"

He smiled and nodded his head several times toward her office window, "She's over there."

Liz sighed, "Let's start dinner."

Over dinner they planned for their next job. Liz will do the family's research while Abigail handles the husband. Margaret will summon the demon. There's always a demon.

Bill will watch the children including the clients' kids.

Alexandra provided security over the entire house.

Bill stretched his arm out, "I'm ready for a good night's sleep."

Margaret cleared the table, "I'll load the dishwasher and I think I'll retire early myself."

"I'm going to run the bath for the girls. I'll see you all in the morning." Abigail pulled Mary Elizabeth's chair away from the table, "Come you, let's head upstairs."

Liz took Bill's hand and squeezed tight, "I'm going to help with the dishes and 'I'll be right up."

Before heading upstairs Liz stopped in her home office, papers and books were scattered on the desk, the lamp faced her family tree.

"Good night Alexandra."

The light flickered. *Always close.*

Upstairs Liz laid her head on the pillow, Bill wasn't kidding when he said he was sleepy. He snored loud and steady. She closed her eyes. Her heart rate increased. The hall light, she thought, maybe she forgot to turn on the hall light. She opened her eyes. The hall

light shown through the door. She closed her eyes. "Just kidding," she whispered and smiled. She opened her eyes again.
　　Darkness.

Made in the USA
Charleston, SC
08 February 2014